THE FANTASY OF LOVE:
THE CAGED HEART

The Fantasy of Love: The Caged Heart

Tshombe

TS Amen Publishing
2019

First Printing: 2019

ISBN 978-0-9832001-6-1

TS Amen Publishing
490 Lake Park Avenue, 10824
Oakland, CA 94610

www.tsamenpublishing.com

Dedication

This story is dedicated to my grandmothers, Bessie Dedrick and Aileen Paterson, who worked most of their lives serving others so that their children and grandchildren could someday enjoy a better life.

Introduction

This book is meant to help those who read it gain a more positive perspective toward being with and remembering loved ones who may have been taken for granted. No one can change the past, but with this read, please know that you can change the future. There is always a way to make things better.

The story of Hope, Faith, and Justice is one that touches all our lives at one point or another. Who in this world hasn't Hoped for something? Who in this world hasn't held Faith in something they couldn't see but knew was there? Who in this world doesn't seek fair and righteous treatment — Justice? In this story I have placed Hope, Faith, and Justice in the same home; with Hope dearly departed, leaving Faith and Justice struggling to continue without her. The name Justice will read "Justus" to connect a deeper humanity to the word's definition. Please rest assured their meanings will remain in the content of their character.

Justus struggles with Faith. We (Justus) seek Faith's redemption through our connection to Hope. We all have a watch over our lives. Faith keeps a close watch, discovering Justus beneath a spike in the twists and turns of life. Do not rob Justus of his Faith. The peace of liberty delivered through Faith shall grant Justus freedom. Observe the record of impressions, shhh...

The Caged Heart

LOSING A DAUGHTER

Justus

My Faith doesn't like being around me. When she's here it doesn't feel like it. Her friends and her life are kept outside. I can't ask a question. I can't read her mind. "Faith," I say. "Faith," I repeat myself and still she doesn't respond. Am I alone in having a daughter who treats me this way? She hates me. I am the problem in her life, holding her hostage with my disability. A crippling disability... My Faith doesn't see it that way. In her words and actions, in her eyes, I did this to myself on purpose. She used to cry for me. As a little girl, she felt sorry for me. Her eyes now show only contempt at any mention of me or us.

My problem: I can't step outside this house without being gripped by fear. I don't want to be around strangers.

She rolled her eyes and stormed off tonight.

I didn't step a foot past the door to chase her. I couldn't. My dog barked at the open barrier leading outside. I listened. The car door opened and closed. The key turned in the ignition. Quickly I ran to the barrier and closed myself in. Her car sped down the long winding driveway away from home.

Arriving here 29 years ago under the cover of night I laid eyes on this place thinking of heaven and blessings. I come from a tough city. Living on land like this only happened in the movies for people like me. Twenty-nine years of living in this house and I've probably been past the front door fifty times. I hate that door and it hates me just the same.

A beautiful woman named Hope rescued me from a life of danger. When I see my daughter, Faith, that beautiful woman is reflected back. How does a man live with a woman who loves him while not loving her? I did. No matter how hard I tried, I couldn't do the romantic things a man should do. I wanted to give her that level of love she deserved, but what I did never amounted to anything meaningful. Last year she collapsed to her death whilst carrying furniture outside. Beyond that cursed door on the dirt covered ground, I watched the woman who rescued me fall and take her last breath. She lay there knowing that I wouldn't venture outside, even to help her. Frozen, I watched from my side of the barrier as medical technicians carried her away. My Faith can't understand how I remained inside while her mother lay dying.

She'd been away at college enjoying life on her own when the voice she wished to escape gave her the news that her mother was in the hospital. She rushed from school to the hospital, then from the hospital to this house. She walked in through that door, her eyes puffy and red from crying. Once inside I rushed to hug her, to give her comfort from the exhausted torment of our loss, but her eyes turned cold and unfeeling at the sight of me. Currents with more tears welled in the corners of her eyes and she put her palm flat against my chest halting my embrace. She snarled and fixed her words through gritted teeth.

"Did you go outside when she fell?"

Caught in my throat the words choked out of my mouth. I stuttered in a failed attempt to explain, excuses, my failure. She rolled her eyes in disgust and walked past me to her room. She slammed the door so hard it sent echoed vibrations through the entire house. Then trying not to be heard, softly, she cried for her mother until sleep claimed her senses. Faith's lived here ever since that night but hasn't made this place her home.

I eavesdrop on her phone conversations, grasping at any way I can to get to know her, to understand her. Tonight was no different than the rest. In my mental depths, I know she moved here to torture me; to punish me for the loss of her mother. I have come to expect this treatment, but it still slices a deep, sharp penetrating pain with every encounter. As a man, I should have been carrying that furniture outside the house. I should have sprinted through my fears past that demon door, in order to assist the beautiful woman who rescued me. The angels in that hospital sent my daughter here to make me feel what I inflicted on the woman who loved me the most. With open arms, I accept my punishment, but I won't reciprocate. My daughter's palm to my chest continues to deny my entry toward redemption, yet still I love her no matter what.

A person's desires should be worth them giving their all. Being disabled holds me back from reaching past fear to acceptance. Trapped in a fortress I've built I'd rather hold onto everything I know right now than go beyond that door. This distrust I created by circumstances once under my control. Tonight, as I walked past her room, I heard her talking. Her voice dancing up and down in melodic tones. The lilt in her speech excited my spirit. My heart fluttered with joy at the sound of her laughter. Stopping at the door, I smiled as I listened. She spoke of "Rob". She always talks about him. As people in love do, she echoed their conversations to the audience on the other end of the phone. She spoke of Rob's latest adventures working for his father's business. She giggled as she told her friend what Rob had asked of her. He wanted to take her on a vacation to some tropical island.

"He knows I can't stay on an island for an entire week." Her voice lowered with an added tone of discretion. "You know why Steph." Whispering even more, "I can't leave daddy during harvest for vacation." There was a pause for her friend's response then, "yeah, yeah… maybe someday, but right now I can't. I have to go Steph. I'll call you later."

I quickly moved away from her door, just moments before it opened.

"Father, what do you want for dinner?"

Trying to please her, "Whatever you cook is fine with me honey."

An arrow sliced through my chest into my heart.

"What I want for dinner can't be made here. I'm doing this for you. We have some pasta, TV dinners… You want that?"

I answered. "Yes sweetheart, that's fine. Thank you."

Another arrow pierced my skin without breaking flesh.

"Don't call me 'sweetheart', it reminds me of Mom."

I tried to get away, but her aim was spot on.

"You always walk away when I mention Mom. I can't stand living here." She snatched her keys off the kitchen counter. "I'm going to pick up something at a restaurant. I don't feel like cooking. I'll bring you something back since what I want is fine with you." Her hands turned the knob and unlocked the latches. "If I take too long just heat up one of those T.V. dinners. I should be back in an hour."

She stormed off, purposely leaving that door open for the dog to follow, "Come here, Watch. Come outside boy. Come on."

He barked at her and held his ground on this side of the door.

"Stupid dog. Make sure he goes outside. He hasn't used the bathroom."

That's how she got into her car tonight. Leaving me here with a body full of arrows, relieved tonight's torture was over.

In bed and I can't sleep. She came home around midnight. I heard the door's telltale creek when she came inside. I always hear that door. She tried to walk quietly but I heard every step. I sniffed to smell if she'd brought home dinner. My insecurities. I hoped with every sniff that the aroma of dinner for me would enter my nostrils. I smelled nothing. I listened for the sound of noise in the kitchen. She went directly to her room. There was a time my little girl would never have acted this way toward me. All I can do now is wish that she will be here in the morning, so I can see her even though she hates me.

HAVING A FATHER

Faith

"Going to check the groves, Dad. I'm gonna take Watch with me. C'mon Watch! C'mon boy! Let's take a walk. That's a good boy. We'll be back soon."

He doesn't even say thank you, Watch. My 64-year-old father. He's not in a wheelchair; he's not physically handicapped. If he were impaired, I wouldn't mind tending to him, but he's not! He just has his *condition*. He's unable to talk to or deal with strangers. He's terrified of new people. Whatever. He chooses to never leave this house or this land. Yet he goes outside once a year during the first few nights of the summer moon; to inspect the oranges for the coming harvest. When Mama lay dying on the ground, he stayed behind that threshold. Had the workers not been here, Mama wouldn't have gotten any help. His phobia is selfish. He's not trying to make sure I have a life. Mama made me promise to take care of him if anything happened to her. Well now she's dead and I am cursed by my promise to her. I hate it.

When I went off to college Watch, I thought I'd reached freedom. As a little girl, I dreamed of living in the city; growing up on a citrus farm with a father who can't go outside, or have anyone over, makes for a stale existence. At the time, Watch, going to college was the first new place for me for a long time. Really for the most part of my life. At eighteen years old, the farthest I'd been from home was Mr Smith's general store for groceries. Leaving this land was a dream come true.

The drive to the college campus overwhelmed my imagination. Looking at different cars going past us was a treat for me. Staring at people walking on the sidewalk held me in tension and suspense, what would they do next? I watched it all in slow motion. Savoring every second, hungering for something new. When we arrived at the end of my dream journey, I stepped out the car to happiness or, so I thought. My first day of college. Of course, Mama drove me there without Daddy. Her face was full of excitement and delight, she wanted me to have a life away from this farm too, yet here I am. The day I left for college all sorts of fantasies danced in my head. The first time I'd ever wake up away from this place. Something different for my life. Something different for my day. But when I hugged Mama, I didn't want to say goodbye. We both held on tight, not wanting to be the first to let go. I held on longer. I hated that she was coming back to this place. I wanted her to stay. She told me not to cry and gently kissed my forehead. She told me she'd be okay. Mama knew the tears from my eyes were not for me. She loosened our embrace to look at me and said,

"Remember everything you learned. Keep home private. Don't talk about the farm. I don't want to upset your father. I love you, honey."

She put another gentle kiss on my cheek. I can still feel her breath on my face. She turned and walked to the car. She didn't look back. I watched as she got inside and drove away. In all my fantasies about the first day at college, my first day away from this place, I never pictured the moment when Mama would walk away. My first day at school I cried myself to sleep.

It took a few weeks before I began searching the computer to find places to go in the city. My roommate was no help. You'd have been more help than her, Watch. After all those years of wanting freedom to move as I please, I wasn't about to stay inside my dorm room. I could study anywhere I want. My very first friend, a girl named Carolyn in my dormitory taught me how to drive. Carolyn is the best. You'd really like her. Mama had told me to make friends at school before making friends in the city. I don't have any friends outside the ones I made at school. Mama would be proud. Carolyn's dorm room was across the hall from mine. We bumped into each other at orientation and became fast friends. Mama always said,

"You meet people in the places you go. So, stay in places that make you happy and you'll find good friends."

Stop all that loud barking, Watch! Mama's words get you all excited, you stop all that yapping. I'm trying to look at these oranges. You know this is my favorite tree. This whole row has the sweetest oranges of the bunch. I remember… You just hush up and listen to my story. Good boy. These don't taste as good as last year. We need to tend to the soil over here; can't tell Daddy about that. That came in handy while I was away at school. I planned everyone's surprise parties. All those things to do in the city, yet city people only see what's right in front of them. If you ask me it's too much going on for 'em. "Beyond all that you've experienced a new experience awaits you." Stop yapping, Watch. I hear Mama too. Let's walk over to the barn and eat some of these oranges while the sun goes down. Remember how Mama used to always call my name during the sunset? Remember, Watch? I could hear her wherever I was on the farm. She'd say, "Faith, Faith honey… Where are you?" I'd say, "Here I am Mama… Here I am." Come on, Watch, I'll race you to the barn. We can sample a few of these oranges. After that we gotta get back so I can cook dinner.

TALKING TO SPIRITS

Justus

My daughter talks to my dog more than she talks to me. I don't speak much while Faith is here. I try to keep my words to a minimum. Most I do for conversation when Faith is gone is click, stomp, whistle, and clap to my bird while my dog watches. My 26-year-old African Grey parrot is like an old record player. I click my mouth, stomp my foot, clap my hands and whistle to make my bird play the old songs of sound made by us living in this house. My parrot, like my dog Watch, has a unique name, Shhh. If I click my mouth twice fast my bird will repeat things said five years ago. A single click of my mouth with a pause takes us one year back. I whistle once for the first full moon of the year. That basically counts the months but there are more than 12 full moons in a year. One whistle starts us at the first moon of the winter. I stomp my foot for each quarter moon. I clap my hands to reference how many days over the quarter moon. If I click my mouth twice fast, whistle my lips once, clap my hands three times and stomp my foot once my great African bird will repeat everything heard in this house for three days over a quarter moon five-years ago last winter. It took over ten years for us to develop and figure out. We still have our lessons and quizzes but for the most part, we have our routine down pat. Other than those clicks, claps, whistles and stomps I don't really have much conversation with anyone. Drunk off whiskey spirits that I make myself. I call his name.

"Shhh…click-click… click… click, whistle-whistle-whistle-whistle-whistle-whistle, clap-clap-clap-clap-clap."

My bird does his dance. He lifts one claw off his perch and puts it down. He lifts his other claw up in the same fashion and puts it down. He lifts his head high to flex his majestic crowning feathers. Then he takes a deep puff of air into his chest.

"Squawk! Come on Mama. We're going to be late. Swees, swees." In a higher, much faster pitch, "I'm coming honey. Swees. I'm coming, honey. Squawk."

I clap my hands loud. Shhh lifts one claw up from his perch and puts it down. He lifts his other claw up and puts it down in the same fashion. He holds his head high and takes another puff of air into his chest. He speaks of the next day from the one I just asked him to repeat.

"Squawk… I hated to leave her there Justus. I hated to leave our baby. Squawk! I should've gone inside. Swoos, I should have gone inside. Swoos."

I decided to let Shhh play that moment out. Unless I blow my breath hard to stop him, he'll repeat the entire day from his memory until there is no more. I gave him his favorite treat. He did his little dance lifting his head and puffing his chest. Wiggling as he chewed his food. He continued with the day as requested.

"Squawk… You couldn't go inside Hope. You had to leave. Swoos. You had to leave. No attention… No attention. Squawk."

The door opened fast. Watch and Faith came in from inspecting the orchard groves. I blew my breath hard to stop Shhh's beak. Watch came straight to me to let me know where he'd been. His breath smelled of oranges, his paws had dust and hay between the pads. Hmmm... Sunset eating oranges at the barn. He sniffed me. He smelled the liquor. He licked my face. Yep… sweet oranges this year. I should've had them instead of the whiskey spirits. My Faith yelled out,

"That bird always brings up bad memories."

She stormed into the kitchen. I closed my eyes and listened. She banged the drawers. She banged the cupboard doors. She was looking for ingredients for tonight's supper. I wondered what the house special would be this evening. Something from the menu of hate-filled surprises as prepared by my loving daughter. Painfully I sat waiting, hoping to savor a hint of love in the meal she prepared. I have yet to taste her loving touch in cooking and preparation. She clinks and bangs the utensils, pots, and pans. I watch her hands trying to understand what, if she receives any pleasure from making these meals for me. I'm her father. She'd rather I talk to spirits or animals than speak lovingly to her. It hurts. I beg for honor, not wanting to offend her power of judgment over me. Hour upon hour she quietly starves me of her love. She carries my blood in her heart. She won't accept my apology. My bird listens and my dog watches as day after day my Faith slowly slips away. I pray to the Holy Spirit, please bless my daughters' heart with forgiveness. I hope that someday may she be in a good place to easily find her way to peace. In grace, we pray... Amen. It's time for dinner.

LISTENING TO THINGS YOU SHOULDN'T HEAR

Justus

Tonight, while eating my dinner she sat on the living room couch and cried. My place at the table allowed us a view of each other. I tried to ignore her sobs. I tried not to hear her sniffles. All I could think is Hope, I miss you; I miss you so much, my wife. You held this house together. You made this family work under such harsh conditions. When you were here this place felt like home. Our bird chirped and squawked all day without worry. Our dog's tail could always be found wagging. Shhh barely chirps while Faith is here and Watch rarely has a reason to wag his tail. For all Hope did I never gave her what she required. Imitating love is not making love because it doesn't sustain the necessary ingredients to complete the recipe for being in love. The formula for synthetic feelings is a lot like the meal my daughter prepared for me tonight. Beans, carrots, pork, squash and brown rice thrown in a pot of cold water waiting to boil, slowly cooked with no spices or salt. The food cooked in some parts and in others it's a soggy mess. Trying to pretend it was enjoyable as I chewed, whilst in agony as my daughter sat in front of me sniffling and crying. Seeing her face covered in tears I could feel the taste of sadness on my tongue. Finally, I got the last bite into my mouth. She stood up from her seat on the living room couch. Staring me down, she walked towards the table. I avoided her puffy red eyes whilst chewing the last rice-crunchy-cold-water-soggy-bite. She reached the table arms folded and stood over me. At that point, she had no sniffles, no cries, just tears down her cheeks. Her words came through fixed teeth as though she were lifting a weight with all her might.

"Are you finished?"

I knew I was on shaky ground having just endured another one of her punishing hate filled meals. Timidly I responded.

"Yes. I'm done Faith, thank you."

She snapped back.

"You don't have to thank me."

She snatched the plate and silverware from the table and stormed off. She stomped her feet and headed to the kitchen. I closed my eyes. She dropped the load into the sink.

"Dang it," she yelled. "I broke another dish." I opened my eyes.

"It's ok Faith. We can get more."

"I don't need you to tell me that. I know if anything around here needs to be done I'm going to have to do it. Did it occur to you that was Mom's favorite china? She bought them before I was born."

I tried to diffuse the situation.

"I'm sorry honey. I, I didn't mean it like that."

"It's not what you said. It's what you don't say and please don't call me honey."

Another bad response. I knew better than to call her honey. How many times does she have to tell me that? What's wrong with me?

"Did you hear me, Dad? I hate when you're drunk. You don't think of or understand anything but yourself. You weren't even listening."

I don't know what she said while I was thinking; I knew she'd be mad if I told her I wasn't listening. So, I clicked my mouth once and clap my hands twice. Saying, "There are mosquitoes in here."

Shhh began doing his dance, He squawked.

"Let's go outside tonight and look at the harvest. Squawk! Look at the harvest.

The fruit should be ripe. Squawk. The fruit should be ripe. Swoosh."

I blew my breath hard.

"Shhh...shut-up bird"

Faith slammed some of the pieces of broken china into the trash.

"I wish you'd let that stupid bird fly away."

I got up from the table and grabbed Shhh's favorite treat, peach pits, and walked over to him.

"It's time for him to go to bed. Let me grab the curtain and cover his cage so he can go to sleep."

"I'm not letting you grab his curtain. You don't have to ask permission." I passed the treat through his cage.

"How about we go outside tomorrow Faith and look at the oranges like old times?"

"I already went out there today. As far as I'm concerned, they are ready for harvest."

She began to move towards her room. I'd failed again.

"You can go out and inspect them if you want. You don't need me." She closed the door behind her.

Wounded and angry, I screamed out the pain of my frustration. Why can't I do anything right?

"Ahhhhhh!"

The glass filled with drink flew from my hand. The liquid transitioned from cup to everywhere.

My aim was spot on. The glass struck its mark against the door that holds me hostage. A thundering clap came from its impact. The thick glass didn't explode, it didn't shatter. Not even a crack. I should've thrown it harder. Another thing I didn't do right. The cup rolled in front of me. I kick it away with all my might. It seemed like the thing to do but now I think why? It flew toward Faith's bedroom door and shattered into countless pieces. That's when I heard her stomps coming. I yelled out, to stop her.

"Baby no!"

Her door swung open. She came out too quick.

"What is going on? Ouch! What the hell?"

She hopped on one leg away from the broken glass in front of her door back onto her bed. I rushed over to help.

"Get away from me!" She screamed, grabbing her wounded foot, I stopped. She continued, "Get me some tweezers. You act like a child. You throw a cup at my door, then scream and yell because I don't want to walk through the orchard? I hate living here with you. All you wanna do is hold me hostage with your condition. You go out at night and look for oranges but when mama needed you..." She stopped. She didn't finish the thought. This is how it feels to be a man who makes his daughter cry almost every day. I handed her the tweezers and wished she'd let me tell her.

"That's not what's wrong, Faith. Let me tell you what the problem is. You've never heard my side of the story."

She looked up from pulling glass out of her foot.

"Tell me what happened? Your side of the story? You think I want to hear why you couldn't run to her side as she lay dying? I don't wanna hear it."

In her beautiful face all I can see is her mother. In all my prayers and apologies to Hope I have never been satisfied because it has always felt pointless. Hope didn't deserve the pain she endured while being with me. Hope my beautiful savior... gone. But looking upon my Faith now gave me the sense for the first time of possible redemption, Hope was still in this house.

"I'm going to tell you anyway Faith. You don't have to accept it. Please just listen and hear me."

She continued to pull pieces of broken glass from her foot. She didn't look up.

"If you think it will make a difference with how I feel then you are wasting your time. I can't help but hear. When I'm finished, I'm leaving whether you're done talking or not."

"My mother's dead and you can't change that."

"I understand Faith."

Silence.

I took a deep breath and begin my first open apology to my family since losing Hope.

"Your mother was an angel to me. Hope held majestic wings in my eyes. I always felt unworthy of her love and devotion. She gave her all to stay here with me in this house under these conditions. She pledged her life to be my wife. Any man would have been lucky to have her. I admit this miserable condition caused me at times to overlook her presence as a blessing in my life. No matter what happened, her actions day to day brought warmth and love to my life. She always spoke from her heart. I pick myself to pieces thinking over moments I wish I could take back, when I was bitter and foolish, when Hope was here. I hate that I gave her day to day this selfish bitter heart."

Faith finished with the tweezers by throwing them on the floor. She hopped on her good foot off her bed. I expected her to close the door. She didn't. I grabbed a broom to move the glass out of her way. I swept a few sweeps and looked at her. She was packing a bag. I stopped sweeping. I knew it hurt but she had to know.

"The day Hope died is a day which haunts me. There are so many things about that day I wish I could change. I wish I would've said my good morning to her. I wish… I would've done more. She gave me so much and I gave her nothing but this condition."

Faith moved frantically grabbing her belongings. My words. My actions. How many times had I made her cry?

"If you think this is helping me or making things better you are wasting your time."

She put the last of her clothes in the bag and zipped it. She hopped over to grab some shoes. A pair of socks already in her hand.

"I always loved Hope. I always will love Hope. There are things we weren't always able to share with you about our life together. We held a lot of secrets Faith."

She looked up from tightening her shoelaces.

"Secrets? Our house is a secret dad. Keeping secrets is all we do here and that's why I hate this place. I'm leaving. Try and get some sleep. You're drunk."

JUSTUS ETCHED IN STONE
Justus

Faith wanted me to sleep. After cleaning up the broken glass in front of her bedroom I sat with my bird, my dog and my whiskey spirits, clapping, clicking, stomping and whistling. Shhh danced as he played the recorded impressions of this house. Eating his favorite treat, we stayed up past his bedtime. My beautiful majestic African-grey-parrot. His facial feathers adorned by the colors of fresh white snow and powder grey gun smoke merging into this swirl of different greys on his marble polished beak. The recordings of this house belt through his twelve-inch frame with a loud piercing pitch. His snow like chest feathers matches his head feathers both of which puff when he speaks. My dog Watch lowers his head every time my great bird sings. Saying my prayers to the spirits out loud again tonight I wept on my hands and knees and asked for forgiveness. No matter how these nights go I always seem to find myself in the pleading position. My beautiful Hope loved me unconditionally. We held hands through many storms in this life and weathered this land together. Our love lives in the veins of our daughter and my beautiful Faith hates the part of her that is me.

I wish I could explain to her the reason why things are not as they seem. So much to say and no way to say it. "Justus!" Shhh startled me.

"Squawk! Squawk! tell her the truth. Just tell her the truth. She's old enough to know. Squawk! She's old enough to know. Tell her the truth. Swoos!"

A few beats out of rhythm the feeling in my heart let me grasp the truth of those words. Shhh didn't dance. He just looked at me as I huddled on the floor. Why had I taken off his curtain after telling him goodnight? He's supposed to be asleep that's why he's acting unusual. I rose from the floor, grabbed his curtain and rushed over to cover him up. His face turned to the left, I could see my reflection moving closer in his eye. He didn't dance. He just stared me down. As I drew the cloak to cover his cage, he raised his head and squawked:

"It's not too late. She's old enough to know. Swoos. She's old enough to know. Squawk."

His name pushed through my teeth hard and loud as I blew my breath, "Shhh, it's time to rest." His cage covered, the house fell silent.

Faith told me she wanted me to sleep. It's been hours since I covered up my bird. I'm trapped inside my thoughts and those thoughts keep me trapped in this house. Sleep rarely finds me. Tonight's loss doesn't surprise me. Did my ears deceive me? Was Hope speaking through my bird? How could that be? I drank a lot after Faith left. She's still gone. I don't want to worry about her. I don't want to dwell too much on the things she's said or my bird's last sentence. The mind can blur dreams and imagination. A man who rarely finds sleep has a tendency to overthink things.

My body is held hostage by my thoughts. Exhaustion finds me but sleep rarely comes with it. Night after night I torture myself with thoughts from my own recorded impressions of this house. Shhh and I have much in common. We don't forget a single moment of our lives. He said, 'she's old enough to know'. I must suppress my thoughts about what has been said and try to focus on something different. Got to get out of bed. Distraction. A carving project I have taken up satisfies my need on a night like this. I ordered a piece of marble a few nights after Hope died. Faith doesn't know. It was going to be a surprise. She'll see I'm not selfish. She'll remember the days as a little girl when my stories mesmerized her to sleep. She'd come running up to me tugging on my clothes. I'd look down into those big beautiful eyes of my little girl, and she'd say, "Daddy its bedtime!"

Hope and I were strict about her television and movie watching. We wanted to protect her or protect us, whatever the case. Faith had very little outside influences, so she couldn't wait for her bedtime story. Until one day ... she was riding her bike, the sun was shining bright, the workers were just arriving. Hope was making some of her famous ice-cold tea in the kitchen. A pick-up truck full of garden tools came to rest in front of the main drive to the property. One of the orchard workers went over and began talking with the driver of the truck. I ducked down out of the window, so they wouldn't see me, but Faith's eyes locked on me as she came speeding around the front of the driveway. She didn't see the truck because her eyes had been locked on me ducking out of view. The talking workers didn't see her. They had no idea she was there. With a loud thunk, she flew over the handlebars of her bike and crashed shoulder first into the hard metal tail bed of the truck. A rake fell loose from the standing garden tools in the bed of the truck. I ran to help her on reflex and instinct but stopped at the front door. I just stopped...at the open door.

"Faith!" My voice screamed out.

The workers looked up at me. My cover blown, I still didn't move past the door. My dazed little girl looked up at me. Her mouth wide open crying out in pain. Her teary red eyes opening and closing, fixed on me. Every time they closed, she cried out louder. The rake didn't do any more damage when it hit her, but the damage had been done. The startled workers were already running before the rake fell. They arrived just as it hit her. I stood at the door frozen. Hope pushed past me.

"My baby!" she screamed, "Justus, stay in the house. Close the door." I heard her through a daze but still stood frozen, paralyzed. Hope turned back, stopping her rush to our injured daughter. "Justus! Close the door. I have to leave. Put the iced tea in the refrigerator. I'll call you from the hospital, stay inside."

She turned back without waiting for me to respond. She ran over to Faith and scooped our daughter up in her arms. Faith's crying eyes fixed on me, still opening and closing as her mother carried her to the car. I closed the door and sat against it on the floor. Still inside the house.

My daughter never asked me to tell her a bedtime story again, and whenever I tried to tell her a story from there on, she'd look… annoyed, roll her eyes and pretend to fall asleep before I could finish. I stopped telling her stories because she didn't want to hear them anymore. The story I carve into this piece of marble is a pretty picture, I know someday she will see and appreciate. Shhh said, "She's old enough to know the truth!" Hope's words. Carving this story into stone reminds me of when Hope and I lived alone. The day I met my friend.

When we moved to this house my condition wasn't this bad. I didn't feel the gripping fear which holds me hostage now. Going outside when workers were around was still a concern. The new land gave me the isolation I needed to not deal with new people. It gave me comfort. No reminders about the life we left in the city. We lived in the country now. Hope woke up with the sun and would tend to the earth each and every morning. I'd read books and surf the internet. When I'd get bored, I'd go for a walk around the orange groves. I wouldn't travel on regular walking paths. I would weave in and out of cover and climb in the trees to watch workers walk past. One day, while I was sitting on a branch, a younger female worker screamed at the sight of me. Startled, I fell. Some male workers unfamiliar to me subdued me, not knowing what happened. Speaking very little Spanish I could not explain. Hope came over and made sense of things quickly. She said 'mi esposo' and the workers loosened their grips. Hope moved and consoled the woman. She calmed the woman with a hug while speaking in Spanish. The workers all apologized, surely in fear of losing their jobs.

"Disculpeme. Lo siento. Disculpeme."

Hope assured them all was ok.

"No problema, no problema."

Their faces eased. My face, tight with embarrassment as I went into the house. Hope wasn't far behind me. To this day I can still hear that worker woman's scream and see the horror on her face as she looked up at me. Hope consoled me.

"Well Justus, you gave that woman a scare. You know how afraid they are of authorities. They all know your face now… I think you should find a better place to eat oranges."

Reaching in the refrigerator I snapped back without looking. "I'm not going to do that anymore. I'll stay inside and watch all of them come and watch all of them go before I'll let someone see me and scream like that again."

Hope came and rubbed my shoulders as I poured a glass of iced tea. I pulled away, she tried again. Her soothing hands always eased my knots of stress. This time I didn't pull away. I drank from the cold glass of her famous iced tea.

"If it makes you happier to stay inside, I will do everything I can to make sure you are at ease with your decision." She kissed me on the cheek. "I love you."

Drinking my tea as her hands soothed me.

"Thank you."

She kissed my cheek again.

"I'm going to start dinner. You hungry?"

My condition worsened that day. I wish it hadn't. Hope wished I'd change my mind but over the years my stubbornness won out. Going out at all seemed pointless. By nightfall, I began to wonder who else or what else awaited me out there. I knew it was safer inside. An environment only changed under my watchful eye but not going outside changed who I was. My heart grew bitter and colder at the world and the growing weight of my cold bitter heart fell on Hope. Smiling as always, she made the most of it.

One day while my frustration about a world news crisis consumed me, Hope came in the house with a strange new object. Of course, being something new in this house meant my instant rejection. Before she pulled the curtain off, I knew what hid underneath the dome shape, outlines of cylinders, of columned pillars, a birdcage. Showing contempt, I tried to ignore it. Hope beamed with excitement as she pulled the curtain off.

"Look what I came across today while in town."

She sat it on the coffee table in front of my seat on the couch. Looking at it I grabbed a peach from a bowl of fresh fruit on the table. She grabbed one too and continued. "He's an African Grey parrot. One of the smartest breeds." She took a bite of the peach. "He doesn't have a name yet."

The bird squawked.

"Shhhhhh, stupid bird!"

I was upset by the startling sound the bird made but after a moment or two of paused silence, I giggled. "That should be his name. Stupid loud bird."

I picked up a book I had been reading before being interrupted by the news flash. Hope didn't even let the remark phase her spirit as she moved towards the cage finishing her peach. I noticed a little fruit left on the seed. She opened the slot to the cage. The bird took the seed from her hand with its beak and crunched it into his food tray. Then he did a little dance.

"*Shhh...*" Hope said. "That's a nice name, Justus. I like it."

I looked up at her bitterly, trying to fight any feelings of happiness flowing within me. Smirking I uttered, "Well, at least it has a name now." Then I pretended to read my book and ignore her and the bird.

"Yes... it's a good name for your bird honey. Don't worry about cleaning up after him or feeding him, I'll do it."

I continued to read my book, not responding. "I'll get your dinner started, while you two get acquainted."

The bird looked at me and squawked.

"Stupid bird," I said.

Hope lowered her head and looked away. She deserved better.

"Does this thing only eat peach pits?" She lit up with excitement at my interest.

"No, he eats all sorts of things. I brought a book on how to take care of him. We can read it together."

"I'd like that," I said, looking into her eyes. She kissed me. And so tonight ends with me carving into this piece of marble, calmed by thoughts of learning how to care for Shhh with Hope. As the sun came around the night sky, I found the touch of sleep.

FAITH'S OBLIGATION TO HOPE AND JUSTUS

Faith

Hey, Watch! Did Daddy let you out here huh? I just needed to have a smoke before I go in... after two days of being gone... Ahhh... I didn't want to leave Rob's this morning. We got into a fight. He wants to know why I won't move in with him. I sounded stupid making excuse after excuse. Even though he did not accuse me of being dishonest I know he wanted to. I asked him if he understood and he said, 'Your dad's waiting for you.' Why does he always say that when we fight? He doesn't understand, and, why should he? I love Rob, Watch. We have been together for some years now yet he's never been to this place. He met Mama a few times and he came to Mama's memorial with me. Just us and the workers. No Dad. He didn't even want to be mentioned. Rob said, 'After being with someone that long, his phobia must be strong to keep him from saying goodbye.' I didn't tell him how father stood by and watched her die. How do I tell him that? If he knew he'd never let me come back to this house. Am I wrong for thinking freedom comes with the death of my father? I feel bad for having thoughts like that about him but sometimes thoughts like that consume me. They run wild. I have moments of clarity but I still wish I wasn't his daughter. I wish he'd go away. I wish I didn't have to come back to this place. It's hard to catch myself when those thoughts come over me Watch... I believe in God and I don't want to be part of the devil's work even though sometimes it feels like my father has been sent from hell. Finding purpose in my work here is hard. I'm going to lose Rob. He can't take much more of this. His love is being held under this indeterminate sentence of me taking care of my father. Rob said, 'I think what you're doing for your father is noble. Most people wouldn't put their entire life on hold to serve someone who can honestly take care of themselves.' He continued with 'I want to stick around and wait to build a family with you, but it feels like your father might live another 30 years and if you decide to leave him after 10 or 20 I may resent you making us wait for something you could have done today.' Then he says he thinks we should take some time apart.

My pleas of 'no' only got a question in return.

"Will you move in?"

I couldn't give him a yes answer with definite terms... He's my dream love Watch. He's everything I dreamed a husband would be... I didn't mean to fall in love or drag him into this. When we met I'd change the subject when talk of family came up. He only met Mama by mistake during senior year of college. The first time Mama saw him she said she knew I'd been bitten by the love bug. Mama and I were sitting in a secluded area of the campus on the side stairs of a closed building off the main path. It was the weekend. Mama and I were talking about my plans for after college. She was saying something when I looked up and saw Rob's face. We looked at each other in the way surprised lovers do. I guess it's like wagging your tail Watch. He said one of his science professors had told him he needed to come in that day to discuss some work. The front doors were locked so Rob went off around the side... where Mama and I were sitting. We later found out he wasn't supposed to be there till next Saturday. We all sat there that day after introductions, talking for an hour or more before Mama had to leave. She quizzed him good before she did though. Stop all that barking Watch! Mama told Rob it was nice meeting him and asked me to walk her to the car. Rob apologized for interrupting. Mama said no problem and told him to give her a hug. She said, 'It's God's will we were supposed to meet.

You didn't interrupt anything. It was nice to meet you.' I'll never forget it Watch. Mama gave him a good hug goodbye. I didn't say anything while she and I walked to the car. She did all the talking about father and the workers and that bird. When we got to the car Mama hugged me with a tight record long hug. This time I lost, I pulled away first. I was too eager to hear her thoughts about Rob. She smiled stroked my hair and said,

"He's a nice boy. I see what your plans are a little better now."

Mama really liked him and that made me love him even more. That was two years ago, and my plans are still on hold. Today, Rob didn't hug me goodbye when I left. He leaned in and kissed me on the cheek. Before I knew it, he'd closed the door. I wanted to beat on the door and beg for a hug, but I didn't.

Watch, I don't know what to do about father's condition, but I have to leave... Losing Rob is not something I'm willing to do. Today, Watch! Today I'm moving out of this house. It's time for me to say goodbye to this place and get on with my life. He's going to have to understand. He's going to have to accept it. I'll keep my promise to Mama and check in on him by phone every day and I will drop by once a week. We will have to hire someone to run the farm, but this is what I've got to do. I'm done with this cigarette, let's go inside.

THE CRACKS BETWEEN FAITH AND JUSTUS
Justus

I watched her coast slowly down the driveway toward the house and was taken back to visions of her riding her bike as a little girl. The way she was driving, I knew she wanted to turn around. She came to a stop just short of where she usually parks the car. She sat for a moment. I watched her take a few deep breaths before she opened the door to get out. I let Watch outside while she was still in the car so she could see something that made her happy about coming to this house. She beams with light when she sees that dog. When she sees me her light dims down to the flicker of a candle in the wind. After finishing her cigarette on the porch, she came inside the house. Watch trailed slowly behind her. He didn't come straight to me like he usually does. He went to her bedroom and scratched at the door. Her eyes were blank. She didn't even say hello when she saw me. My dog's actions told me my Faith had still not come home. A person Watch didn't recognize walked with him into this house. "Squawk! We are strong. Squawk! We are strong... Swoos."

He didn't do his dance. He didn't raise one claw. Was this his way of clicking, stomping, clapping and whistling to make me remember the recorded impressions in this house? Those words gave me flashbacks. We are strong... Hope's words.

"Squawk! We are strong" He said it again. Faith stopped walking towards the kitchen. She didn't turn around. She just stopped with her back to me. The house went eerily silent except for Watch's scratching on her bedroom door. I barely heard her words over the scratching. She mumbled with a clenched jaw and tight teeth.

"I'm tired of being in this house."

Her fists balled up and I couldn't see her face. My fear of the situation grew. I blew my breath hard and prayed for my bird not to make another sound, but to my horror, he began to do his little dance. His chest puffed with air. He held his head high and said,

"Faith, we are strong! Swoos."

She turned around. A flash in the blink of an eye. Her constricted pupils made her look like a possessed woman in need of an exorcism. My eyes filled with aplomb and my heart fluttered. Maybe it wouldn't be as bad as I expected. Faith took away the protective covers over my delusions of the truth and at that moment, my fear outmatched my courage. She screamed,

"I hate you! I hate that bird! I hate this house! I hate being here, I hate seeing you!!"

She moved towards me fast and hard. I tried to catch her eyes because my mouth could not plead but her eyes were focused on something beyond me. The bird. The venom in her rage struck past me. My old body crashed on the hardwood floor. She grabbed the cage and threw it to the ground. Shhh flapped his wings in the burst of commotion. Finally, my courage surpassed my fears.

"FAITH!"

Her hands gripped the bars of the bird's confines, banging it and slamming it on the floor.

"I hate this bird!" She screamed, "I hate this bird!"

"FAITH!" I screamed again.

This time she looked up tears trickling off her cheeks.

"What! What do you want? What do you want from me? I have given up everything for you. What more do you want!?"

"The… the bird didn't do anything wrong Faith. Please, please let go of his cage. He's scared."

She looked at him flapping his wings and released her grip of the bars. Through the tears on her beautiful face, a blank stare of revelation emerged giving her a new look of calm. Something of peace. She closed her eyes and exhaled.

"Dad I can't stay here with you anymore. I have got to go. It's time for me to leave."

Slowly, Faith stood and picked up the cage. Shhh fluttered as she put it back on its stand. Then she took a deep breath and came over to me. I looked at Shhh. His feathers flustered as he puffed his snow-white breast.

"Here dad, take my hand. I'm sorry I knocked you down."

"It's ok." I reached out my hand and felt hers for the first time in years. It felt so good to hold her and then the warmth of her touch vanished as a sharp pain shot from my leg to my pelvis. "Ah! Let me go, Faith. It hurts too much to move."

She let go of my hand and shook her head slowly from side to side. Starting at her forehead she pushed the disheveled hairs out of her face. She exhaled. "What do you want me to do?"

I didn't want to say anything to upset her.

"Are you able to move your leg at all? "

"I think I can. It hurts pretty badly Faith, but I'll try to move it."

The mere adjustment of my body to reach out my hand again sent a death gripping agony from my leg to my pelvis. I needed to be strong. I didn't cry out. I held it in.

"I don't think it's that bad. If I can just get to the couch and lay down, I'm sure it will be ok. Let's try again but ease into it this time. It'll work, just help me up."

She bent down and I put my arm around her neck. Just that slight movement caused more unbearable pain. Wishing I had a better tolerance I cried out.

"Put me down. I'm not ready to move yet. Let's just wait a minute."

I unhooked my arm from her neck and went back down the few inches I'd lifted off the floor. More unbearable pain shot through me, but I didn't let her see it. She sat down against the wall facing me and pushed her hand through her hair again.

"Do you mind if I smoke in here dad? I need a cigarette."

She'd already removed a single from her pack.

"I don't mind. Do you have an extra one? It's been a long time since I had a smoke."

She tapped the cigarette pack against her hand and removed another single.

"Do you need me to light it for you?" She asked matter-of-factly, lighting her cigarette and then lighting mine. We were separated by only a few feet. I reached out to meet her halfway, eager to inhale a cool soothing smoke. Faith carried the same brand as her mother. I was reminded of the first time I smoked with Hope. A thick puff of relaxing inhalation filled my lungs. I hadn't smoked in 5 or 6 years. When Hope quit I did too. Faith exhaled and ran her fingers through her hair again. She always did the hair stroking habit when she had something she didn't know how to say, but this time it seemed to come easily. The words rolled off her lips.

"Dad I have to move out. I can't stay here anymore."

I took a deep breath of smoke and exhaled.

"Yeah Faith. I know…."

Exhaling the pressure, she looked relieved.

"Dad this is too hard on me. I have a life outside this house and I want to live it. You're just going to have to learn to do it on your own. I can't keep doing this. There are a few recipes Mama left in the kitchen. You can get your dinner ready. I've seen you cook before."

I inhaled as much smoke as I could and held it in, maybe too long before blowing it out. The lightheaded rush came that I'd been looking for.

"I can cook. I've wanted to cook for you but was unsure if was ok. I can manage."

She ran her fingers through her hair again.

"We need to get Dr Keeler over here to take a look at you."

She got up to get her phone. She'd put it by her keys on the coffee table when she came in the house.

"Let me know when you're done with that cigarette, so I can throw it out.

I took in a puff, no more head rush.

"Here… I'm done now."

She took the cigarette while listening for Dr Keeler to answer the phone

"Hey, Doc… It's Faith. Yeah, Hope's daughter. Hi, yes, I've been good. I know… This world will not be the same without her. No, I'm back from school living here with Dad. That's why I'm calling. We had an accident. He fell. Can you come over and take a look?"

My thoughts were consumed with the possibilities of 'what if.' Watch came back into the room as Faith got off the phone.

"Dr Keeler will be here within the hour. He said he needs to check on someone else before he comes but it shouldn't take too long. He told me not to move you. Do you need anything?"

Watch sat down next to me. I hesitated my answer. Shhh looked at me with his right eye.

"Faith. There's a lot I have to tell you. It's time you knew the truth why your mother and I moved here from the city."

"The truth?" she sighed shaking her head and rolling her eyes.

"Yes, Faith. The truth."

She sat back down against the wall and ran her fingers through her hair.

"Please be done by the time Dr Keeler gets here. I'm going into town after he checks on you."

"Alright, Faith. It shouldn't take too much time."

JUSTUS AND THE JEWELS OF SOCIETY

Justus

Watch walked over to Faith. A gesture from him letting me know Faith was home. Shhh did his dance without saying a word and turned his back on us to face the window. A view for him that looked at the orchard. Her beautiful hand stroked Watch's fur. He licked her face. My words came out.

"When I lived in the city I ran with a bad crowd. The crowd I ran with took the place of my family. Well... there wasn't much of a family. Only me and your grandmother. I never knew my dad. No aunts or uncles that I'm aware of. Drinking is how I remember my mother. Those spirits I make remind me of my time with her. This is why the crowd in the street meant so much. They were all I could depend on for moral support and understanding. When I asked your grandmother questions those questions were met with ridicule or 'shut up I'm busy'. Questions to my friends were always met with answers even if those answers weren't correct. After a while sleeping at your grandmother's house stopped feeling like home. Being awake all night running through the streets causing mischief with my friends took the place of my dreams. At thirteen I found myself addicted to breaking the law. That's about the time I met this girl."

Faith looked up at me. Her eyes softened. I knew what she thought but that wasn't it.

"This girl, at thirteen years old… already seemed like a mature woman. She was responsible and disciplined, not giving in to pressure from our peers. A far away example than what I was used to. Where we lived was rough Faith. Murders, prostitution, assaults, robberies, and drug deals ran reckless through the streets of our neighborhood. Being crazy out there held power and like a plague, you never knew who'd be crazy next. At twelve years old, I'd already seen two murders and countless other crimes. Seeing the most upsetting thing you could think of held no shock to me by the time I was a teen. Hell, I've seen a guy raise a lion in a two-bedroom apartment. Imagine hearing a lion growl next door."

Faith broke a smile. It reminded me of when she was a little girl listening to my stories about the city before bedtime. Her favorite was about the lady in the window who painted her face white to wave at the people as they passed by her house. Every Monday through Friday at 5pm this woman's face would appear in the third story window of an apartment building by our freeway exit. My mom would pick me up from elementary school after she got off work, and every time we got off the freeway, the lady with the white paint on her face would be there. At first being afraid kept me from looking at her. I was only 8 years old and I didn't understand. Then, one day I found myself looking without fear. I caught her eyes. She waved at me and I waved back. The next day anticipation to see her again held me in suspense. I prayed my mother wouldn't stop at the grocery store and she didn't. We got off the freeway right on time and there she was. Looking into my eyes and waving at me. My heart skipped beats with excitement and I feverishly waved back. From that day forward without a word spoken between us we became friends. Every time we got off the freeway after school, I looked forward to seeing her. No matter how bad my day she made me smile. The ritual between us became so common I waved one day before noticing she wasn't there. I thought maybe she was late, or I was early and so the next day came and again the same thing. She wasn't there. A few days later there was a candlelight vigil and that's when I found out, she had died in her sleep. The story got out in the newspaper about why she painted her face white and waved in the window every weekday at 5pm. It was the usual time her husband arrived. He had died 10 years before her on his way home from work. The woman in the window had refused to go to his funeral stating that if she did then he'd really be dead. She never left her house again because she didn't want to miss him when he came home.

My Faith had always enjoyed that story and she was listening to me again as she did back then.

"Yeah, guys had lions and all sorts of things in the city. It was a crazy place. The girl who loved me saw something past all the imperfections in my life. I don't know how she saw beyond the foolishness in the world around us. As messed up as I was, I thought I was doing the right thing by society. In her eyes, my character was greater than the ways I displayed at the time. She saw past my attempts to project a facade that protected me in a place where the weight of good and evil destroyed some people.

Faith got up. "I think I hear Dr. Keeler coming. I'ma go look and see if that's him."

Watch didn't go over to the window. And no cars drove onto this land without him seeing who they were. She knew that. Her going to the door meant something was being said that she needed a break from hearing. Shhh turned his head toward Faith to put her in his right eye.

"Squawk! Swoos!" He flapped his wings and turned back to looking out the window. Watch walked up and licked my face. I stroked his golden fur. Such a good dog. I've had other dogs before. All different breeds seeming to carry the same spirit. Hope used to say, "It seems like that same soul keeps following you."

Every time I look at him the same spirit can still be seen. More to myself than Faith I said,

"The first dog I ever had was named Watch."

Faith turned back from looking out the window and gave me her attention saying, "I guess that wasn't the doctor. You said you had other dogs named Watch before?"

"Yeah... I... my first dog's name was Watch."

She shook her head as she walked back towards me.

"Dad are you okay?"

"Yes Faith, I'm okay."

She sat back down against the wall. Shhh flapped his wings and Watch stayed next to me.

"My first Watch was given to me by a buddy named Grim. 'Grim' was short for Grim Reaper. He gave me a red and white pit bull puppy with a red nose. The puppy looked like it wore a red coat with white gloves and a t-shirt. I loved that dog. Grim was probably 30 or 35 at the time and lived with his mother. He raised dogs and was famous in our neighborhood for street boxing. Most of the kids in our neighborhood would be at his house learning how to fight. I was practicing in his garage when one of his dogs had puppies. At 17 years old and fresh out of juvenile hall I really felt like having a dog to take care of was the thing to do."

A faint smile appeared on Faith's face.

"When I got my puppy home your grandmother told me to get it out of the apartment. We argued. She had been drinking. She tried to grab the dog. I knew if she got hold of the dog, the puppy would have hell to pay. Somehow in the middle of me trying to keep her away from the dog, she fell. In her drunken, deranged madness she'd sworn I'd pushed her. Finally, the day she… the day we'd always known was coming. The day she threw me out."

"Grandma put you out at 17 because of a fight over a dog?"

I closed my eyes and nodded.

"Do you mind getting me a pillow for my head, honey?"

"No, I don't mind." She didn't curse me for calling her honey. She got up to get the pillow. Shhh turned and looked back with that right eye. He stared for a moment and then turned back towards the window. Faith came back with the pillow and placed it gently beneath my head.

"Is that okay Dad? Shouldn't be long before doc gets here. Do you want another smoke or something to drink?"

"No honey, I'm ok."

She removed a cigarette. "Do you mind if I smoke again?"

"No honey, I don't mind." She lit it and took a drag.

"I'd like to say I saw your grandmother's apartment again, but I can't. When I walked out of there it was for the last time, and one of the last times I'd see her. No longer would I call that place home. "

Faith exhaled slowly. She looked down and avoided my eyes. The first truths about her grandmother she'd ever heard. I'd always avoided talking about this and knowing how much more I had to say made me keenly aware of why I'd waited so long to do it. This story was so hard to tell and even harder to have lived.

"Being out in the streets on my own was not as fun as I thought it would be. Somehow, under the delusions of teenage thinking, I pictured the limitless things which could be done instead of what I'd truly have to do."

I motioned for a cigarette. Faith took one out and lit it for me off the one she was smoking.

"I had a buddy named Spike who lived a few blocks away from your grandmother. Spike was a cool kid whose mom spent a lot of time away from home. His mom would be gone for days at a time. Wait, let me back up. Our neighborhood group… we called ourselves 'The Cool Kids'. Spike's mom's apartment served as a regular meeting place for us to gather. When I moved there the group began dropping by more often. This is where my euphoric delusions peaked out of control. I went from my mom's house to my friend's mom's house and in my mind, I believed I was living on my own. The Cool Kids were known around the neighborhood for stick-up robberies. To be a Cool Kid you had to show no fear. 'Cool Under Pressure' was our motto. We tested our potential candidates before making them official members. All you needed to do to be a member was stick up a grocery store or a gas station or something while one of us watched from a distance."

Faith's mouth opened wide with a gasp.

A puff from my lungs into the world, before I continued.

"When I say the word 'all' regarding robbing a store it's because there were groups who did worse things for initiations. Making light of pulling weapons on people isn't what I mean by 'all'. There is nothing cool about that lifestyle. Being a crazy, hurting, mixed-up, delusional kid, it seemed being that way was the only option. Only it wasn't. One day the sheriff taped a notice on the door at Spike's mother's house. We were hanging in the street when the sheriff pulled up. Of course, at first, we thought it was about the robberies. I told the fellas not to panic cause seeing the Sheriff's actions I knew what it was. As soon as the sheriff drove away, we ran to the door. The closer we got to the fourplex building the clearer the word on the notice became: EVICTION. My life changed a lot that day. All my teenage delusions about life on my own were coming into focus with the word: EVICTION. Two months later I found myself living couch to couch at anybody's house who would keep me and my Watch. During that time, I turned 18."

My cigarette was almost finished. I savored the taste, and I didn't want it to end, but I wanted this story to, I just wanted to move forward and never look back. Doing that has always allowed me not to feel what I've done. No reflection. Shhh flapped his wings and looked back at me over his shoulder. A signal. I continued.

"The girl, the woman who stood by my side during this time of adolescence was named Liberty. Her place in this world played the part of her name as perfect as perfect could be. She had to be a Liberty to try and rescue me."

Faith's lips pursed her eyes rolled away. She sighed and blew out the last puff of her cigarette. I took the last puff of mine.

"Liberty loved me despite me not loving myself. As foolish as I was she sensed more in me than I could see in myself. We had this big fight at her uncle's house. There was a Cool Kid job me and Spike had to do. The only reason I'd gone to Liberty's uncle's house that day was to drop off Watch. She begged me not to go on the job and said she'd give me the money I needed if I'd just stay with her and not go. At the time I thought how could she possibly get me the money I needed? She worked part-time at a delicatessen and her always-out-of-work uncle took most of the money for bills. In my mind, it didn't make any sense. Plus, I didn't want to depend on anybody to support me. Even though armed robbery wasn't a decent way to earn a living. Thinking back, I wish I would've listened to her. Instead, I pushed past her as she pleaded for my deliverance from evil. I left her crying on the floor. She kept Watch for me while I was gone.

"The job that evening was supposed to be easy. My buddy Spike had made the plans. It was his move. I needed it bad, but he needed it worse. He and his mom were homeless staying in various shelters around the city. He came to me with this plan of robbing a jewelry store. Spike had heard his uncle talking about the jewelry store owner being stupid for thinking nobody knows why he leaves early. The owner always left right before closing. His uncle said the jewelry store owner left with a ton of cash every day. To confirm what he heard Spike followed the jewelry store owner after work and as expected the trail ended at the bank. As far as we were concerned that validated his uncle's story. We sat outside the jewelry store that evening in a stolen car I'd picked up the night before. The windows were tinted which lowered the chances of descriptions. Spike was real jumpy while we waited in the car. He wasn't acting cool. An old man came out of the store. Spike was like, 'There he is. There he is. Drive, drive.' Our plan had been to pull up alongside the jewelry store owner, force him into the car, and get him to give us the money he had on him plus anymore he might have hidden anywhere else. We didn't have a plan on how to get the information out of him. We just figured he'd see the gun and out of fear for his life tell us where the money was. We pulled up alongside him. Spike jumped out, forced the old guy into the back seat of the car got in behind him, and closed the door. I drove off. From there we got on the freeway and headed to the secluded, industrial part of the city. Out of nowhere while driving on the freeway Spike started hitting the old man. That wasn't cool. That wasn't our style. We were the coolest stick-up kids the city had ever seen. Cool Kids always said, 'thank you' and we never injured people. That was our trademark. I told Spike to knock it off. He didn't respond at first to my commands. Reaching back with my right arm I grabbed him and told him to cool it. That seemed to snap him back to reality. He said, 'The old bastard only has one roll of money. He's holding out. I'm gonna waste his ass if he doesn't tell us where the rest of it is.'

"The jewelry store owner cried out for mercy. This marked the first and only time I'd ever felt remorse on a job. The roll of money was probably a few thousand dollars. In the past, that amount of money would have been enough."

Watch walked over to Faith. She looked uneasy. Her hands had pushed through her hair three or four times. Watch seemed to calm her down.

"We parked behind this abandoned warehouse where we could keep our work private from witnesses. The sun had inched its way down, but light could still be seen haunting the sky. I wish I could have seen the sunset with Liberty that day. Sitting in the car behind the building I wanted to turn around and call the whole thing off, but it was too late. I had a disguise of just a hat and sunglasses. I looked from the rear-view mirror. Spike struck the old man's face with the gun. 'Tell us where the rest of the money is old man!' At first, the store owner told him the rest of his money was kept in the bank but after a few more blows from Spike, the old guy said he did have some money at his store. Spike wanted to drive back right then. He hit the store owner real hard and said, 'Where are the keys to the store old man?!' Spike was out of control. The store owner said he doesn't keep keys on him. His daughter opens the store with a security guard every morning. I asked Spike to get out of the car so we could talk. We got out of the car. I wanted to bring some calm and work out all the kinks in this plan. We needed to figure out How to get into the jewelry store without alerting the guard or hurting anybody else... a logistical nightmare. Looking back, I see we were in way over our heads and had just gone too far. During our discussion, the jewelry store owner got out of the car. Spike grabbed him. They struggled. A monstrous look took shape in Spike's eyes as they struggled. Before I could move to stop it... Bang! Bang! Two shots in the old man's head. I threw up. After cursing and yelling at Spike, who didn't show any remorse, we put the old man's body in the trunk of the car. Then we drove back to an alley wiped the car down and walked away into the night. The only person I could think to call came and met me down the street from where the car was left. She had Watch. I hugged her so tight and didn't want to let her go. She took one look at me and said, 'What have you done?' I told her the truth. 'I didn't do it.' She asked, 'Didn't do what?' I didn't answer her. We went to a motel room and I promised her no more jobs, and no more Cool Kids. I meant that, and, in the morning, I went looking for a job, a real job, and registered for night school. To this day that old man's face still won't leave me alone."

Faith looked up from petting Watch. There was a seriousness about her face that made me feel insecure.

"Did you keep the money?"

"No. Honestly I forgot all about the money. Spike came looking for me at one of the places I usually stayed, I told the people to tell him I wasn't there. I don't know if he came by to give me money and really, I don't care. A coffee shop hired me part-time to sweep up and clean. Night school had just started, and I'd made enrollment. The cops found the old guy's body after about a week and began turning up the heat in the neighborhood. My buddy Grim who gave me my first dog came by the coffee shop and told me Spike had been bragging around town that he'd wasted the jewelry store owner and that I was with him when he did it. My blood boiled with anger hearing that. He killed that poor old man for nothing and had the nerve to boast about it. After work, I went looking for him around the neighborhood. I found him getting high in an alley with some heroin junkies. I pulled him to the side and told him to stop talking stupid, boasting and bragging about killing the old man. I don't remember him saying anything he just started laughing so I just started punching him. He reached for his gun. I grabbed it from his hand and threw it across the alleyway. Blazing hard fists of fury, I beat on him and beat on him until some cops pulled me off."

I signaled Faith for another cigarette with a few taps to my lips from my index and middle finger. She lit one for me and then one for herself.

"I hadn't changed my life for more than a few weeks before I found myself inside an interrogation room with two cops. The first thing one of the cops said was, 'We're investigating the murder of a jewelry store owner in the neighborhood. You got anything you wanna tell us? I sat stone-faced, still pumping off the anger from Spike. He wasn't a cool kid. I'd known him since fifth grade. The smaller cop said, 'We got the gun kid. The buddy you beat up is telling us everything. He says you did it and your prints will be on the gun when we test it. You can keep quiet if you want but I suggest you start talking.' All my mind could fathom at that moment was 'I'm going to go to prison'. I touched the gun. My hands weren't on the trigger but that didn't matter. The only thing the cops needed was my prints on that gun and Spike's statement naming me as the trigger man. The code of the street ran through my veins. I had to abide by the code. No matter what Spike said I couldn't, wouldn't say a word. When the tears fell from my eyes I had no idea the cops would use my tears as evidence in court. Crying after being accused of a crime is an admission of guilt."

"Liberty came to visit me within two days of my arrest. Seeing her eyes, her lips, her face, brought me joy. I'd been dying to know how my dog was doing. She told me she'd take care of him as long as she had to. My heart skipped over so many beats while she spoke that day. Looking at her through thick double glass talking over a telephone hurt. I ached to feel her soft skin on mine. The thirty-minute visit went by too quickly. We pressed our hands against the thick glass like in the movies. Why didn't I listen to her that night and not go on the job with Spike?"

My cigarette had almost found its finish. Shhh now faced us with his head dropped, sleeping. I asked Faith to cover up his cage. As she did so I kissed the smoke goodbye.

"Dad, I'm going to get a drink. Want one?"

I exhaled hard and heavy. The spirits…

"Yeah Faith I'll have one. Could you bring me the bottle of whiskey under the sink? I made it this morning. It's good stuff. Want some?"

She shook her head no.

"That whiskey you make is too strong, Dad. All I want is a glass of wine. I'll get you the whiskey and a shot glass."

"No, need something bigger. The sniffer please."

"Okay, Dad."

She rumbled around in the kitchen and within moments brought back the glasses and bottles. As I poured, the memories of the trial began to haunt me. Faith sat down against the wall. She sat the wine bottle next to her and poured a glass for herself. I took a big gulp of whiskey that cruised harshly down my throat, I needed that.

"During my trial, your grandmother came to what court appearances she could with Liberty. Mom wanted her baby to know she believed him. Your grandmother knew I wasn't a murderer. The trial lasted four days. The big detective testified. The cops who broke up the fight testified, the witness who'd seen two boys running from the car testified. The forensic expert testified about my prints on the gun... Spike testified."

Another gulp of the strong and harsh whiskey.

"Spike received four years in prison for testifying against me. He didn't look at me during his testimony. I was collateral damage. He'd murdered a man, blamed me for it, and got four years in prison. They spared me the death penalty and gave me life without the possibility of parole. At the time I wondered which was better. It only took three hours for the jury to find me guilty. These hardworking people who knew nothing about making a living off the streets found it very easy to decide the rest of my life. Why should they have considered a guy like me innocent? The detectives wouldn't charge an innocent man with a crime. As far as they were concerned, I had to have done something. Spike seemed honest and truthful."

Another gulp for the tears.

"Faith, these are not assumptions I made up about the jury. These are the statements I heard jury members say in chambers. The court locked me in the same stairwell the jury used for accessing chambers during recess and deliberation. I wished I would've had the courage to yell at them behind the door separating us, 'I am innocent!' But my fears didn't allow me to yell. A man accused of murder yelling he's innocent behind the door didn't seem like a good idea. To this very day, I wished I would've. I had nothing to lose.

"The day of my conviction happened on a Friday. A bell sounds and a red light goes off when a jury reaches a verdict. Based on which deliberation room is in session the bailiffs know who to get from a holding cell. I still believed and held hope the bell from the jury room rang to exonerate me of this crime I did not commit. I smiled walking to the elevator. I remember thinking, 'In moments all of this would be over'. The old guard who escorted me from the holding cell to the courtroom carried the face of a pallbearer. Why wasn't he smiling? I thought. It was a good day. I'd return home to Liberty and start a family. I told the bailiff to smile. He tried but his face wouldn't do him the justice. Poor guy, I thought. He's never seen a miracle before."

My baby girl's eyes fixed on me with the softness of a newborn kitten. After all these years she gave me the look I'd missed so much. The expense of receiving such a reward worth the price of telling this painful story. Her look, that look was worth any price to me.

"I was seated next to my publicly appointed, overworked attorney. The small, nervous, little man had probably seen hundreds of misguided youths seated in this position. I was a 20-year-old man at the time of the verdict. Two years of preparation for trial the standard in a case of murder. The judge called the jury into the courtroom and he told me to stand and face them. None of them looked me in the eyes. Still, I felt confident they'd seen my innocence. The court clerk read the verdict. Even as the clerk's words sounded loud and clear I still thought I'd be freed. I thought the clerk must have read the verdict wrong. *Guilty.* The clerk made a mistake. I looked back at Liberty. Then it hit me. The truth of what was taking place. It was over. My heart sank into the bottom of my stomach. The tears melted from Liberty's closed eyes. Guilty! Guilty! Guilty! One by one each juror had to say it for the court record. When the 12th juror said guilty the judge thanked them for their public service. He said something to me, but I wasn't paying attention. The bailiffs took me away. Numb to the world I walked in a daze almost completely unaware of my surroundings."

The gulps of whiskey were taking effect. Burnt this batch from rotting bananas, strawberries, pineapples, granulated sugar and corn syrup rotting in a vat of potato mash. A craft I'd learned in prison. More relaxed I positioned myself to lay flat on my back. I sat the empty sniffer on the floor. I didn't need it. I gripped the bottle and continued with the story.

"My return to the county jail came late. People in trial come back later than the rest of the inmates from the court. The sheriff's deputies with whom I found familiarity in passing already knew the news about my conviction and so their facial expressions showed sorrow upon our contact. I heard some officers say things like 'poor kid, or 'that's too bad' as I passed by. Once I reached the cell block, the guys I knew in jail greeted me like it was just another day. 'Hey boy! How's everything going in court? Did the jury come back yet?' Their words rolled right off me. To this day I don't know if I answered them or mumbled something that I thought answered their questions. I just wanted to go back into the cell and be alone. Once I got there, I laid on my bed and let some tears fall. I heard the others talking in the recreation room. 'He got found guilty?' 'That's messed up.' 'Y'all know he didn't do it. I know who did but I ain't snitchin.' Not much laughing went on in the rec room that night. The fear of conviction loomed over all of them. That day it had been me to feel the crashing rein of the gavel's conviction. Tomorrow, next week, next month, next year, someone else would be in my place... that night I played a part that must happen every day in a civilized society.

"The next morning, I summoned the strength from within to get out of bed. Cell releases to the rec room were done every hour on the hour. At the first unlock at 7am, I walked in a daze to the collect phone and dialed the familiar number. Her voice came on... "Hello." Something in me said I should hang up. There's this recording that plays after she answers the phone it asks will she accept the collect call charges. My hands perspired on the receiver. I took it away from my ear with my fingers gripped tight on the mouthpiece. I hung up before she could accept the charges. A few trickles of pain from my eyes dotted my chest. My shirt absorbed the fresh tear stains. Three or four drops marked the meaning of so much suffering. The way I felt at that moment, an ocean of tears couldn't have expressed. Since then I have created buckets of tears and still I haven't gotten to a point where the pain has been fully expressed. My fingers reached for the buttons again; in slow motion I pressed each number... My heart terrorized its place in my chest as the phone rang. A reflex hearing her voice jerked the phone away from my ear. I almost hung up again. The recording played, asking her to accept the charges. It was hard to breathe waiting for her decision. More and more tears fell on my shirt. The recorded voice said, "thank you" and patched her through.

"She said, 'Hello? ...Hello?'

"At first no words could push through the lump of air blocking my throat. The words I was able to form passed the lump only to turn into cries. My everything in life held the other end of that line and I couldn't speak any words. It was more than a blockage in my windpipe. It hurt. All my dreams of a meaningful life with Liberty were gone.

"On the other side of the phone she said, 'Justus are you ok?' Her voice sounded of blissful peace. My heart calmed and eased the tension in my throat. In the midst of a weep and whimper I found part of my voice and said, 'No, I'm not ok...I don't want you to visit me anymore.'

"She cried out, 'Justus... Justus...' But the words she sang I had to cut short.

"'Don't talk, just listen.' She knew by the tone I meant business. The silence pained the acknowledgement. I said, 'I've got to fight this fight. I'm not going to drag you down with this. You deserve better. You're a good woman Liberty and you're going to make some man very, very happy. Always know, you are the woman of my dreams and know in my dreams I will always find you. I love you more than my life.'

"All she got out was 'Justus...' I ended the call in the middle of her cries. After I hung up I buried my face into folded arms and rained tears over the recreation telephone for almost five minutes. How many other innocent men had stood at that phone to make that call? Pride helped me keep the weak sounds of sobbing close to my chest and the lump was able to form again in my throat."

Watch jumped up and barked as he ran to the window. The doctor had arrived. Dr. Keeler and Hope met many years ago when the good doctor began his senior year in high school. Hope read an advertisement posted on the message board of the general store requesting a tutor skilled at the senior high school level in a multitude of subjects. She pulled the ad down and brought it home. There was a real draw for her to that message. Education didn't mean work for Hope, it was a passion that she truly enjoyed. A request for a tutor meant some young person needed help. Senior high school student Keeler became Dr. Keeler through the encouragement of Hope. We'd only been in town four or five years when Hope had adopted the future doctor. She'd worn one of her prettiest dresses to the graduation and said in simple terms after attending the ceremony. "That is what it's all about." After all the years of work and the young man's progress from high school student to doctor just a few words summed it all up. Dr. Keeler was raised in a single parent home that consisted of a father who worked as a handyman around town. His mother had passed away a few years before we met them. The loss of his mother caused his grades to slip. Dr. Keeler's father didn't have a lot of money. The man wanted his boy to have an education so badly he offered his before and after work services in exchange for his son's lessons. Dr. Keeler's father showed me things around the house to monitor, change, and repair. In some regards I may now qualify as a carpenter, plumber and electrician. A general handyman. When the older Keeler retired he told me if I ever needed his advice or assistance to just pick up the phone and he'd help me as best as he could. Sometimes I call him to troubleshoot but we both know it's my way of saying hello. Dr. Keeler and his father have been our lifeline during our stay here. Trusting people to work in my home around my family isn't something I consider matter of fact. A strange person entering your home should be viewed as cautiously as the body views a germ entering its domain. Some germs are harmless, and some germs are not. Dr. Keeler, the once young senior high school student was here again to make a house call free of charge.

CHAINS AND SHACKLES
Faith

The door to the house is open right now and I feel just like Dad. I don't want to go past the threshold of this house. My feet are like heavy weighted cinderblocks. Walking through the front door to go outside shouldn't be so hard. The world looks different, but I can't allow it to hold me back.

"Come on Watch, we have to go and get this prescription filled. Mangey looking old dog. You need a bath. Get in boy, good dog. You know you're my best friend, right? Did you know that already? Huh? That's my good boy.

Looking at you with your tail wagging and that slobbering tongue seems like you already know dad's story. Did you know about this dog? Stop all that barking. I'm trying to drive. Do you want us to crash? I didn't think so. Yeah…everybody knew but me. The whole house knew. Wonder why the stupid bird didn't say anything? You know what watch? I think that annoying bird was mad at me for knocking his cage down. I put his water back and fixed his food. Spoiled old babbling bird. Anyway, I see dad a lot different now. His trauma with trusting friendships. Spike turned on him. Seems like dad really trusted him. He went to jail for murder? In all my years of seeing him in this condition, I never imagined he could have had an experience like that which put him in the place where he avoids going outside... How horrible. Sitting day after day fearing people; the happenings outside. A distrust turned into a phobia and I'd never thought of his reasons why. We judge people on what we think we know and, in some ways, we compare their lives to our own. We see them doing what they do and from those things we apply our relative understanding. In one of my college classes, I learned that people shape images of things they see to match images of things they have seen before. Why do we see something new and try to make it into something we already know all about? Sounds crazy huh silly dog? Since your tongue's still hanging out of your mouth, I guess that means you're still listening. Watch, most of us humans see people and we judge them based on our understanding of what we have seen or heard before. I viewed dad like that and today he looks like someone new. But he's still the same person. I just have a different perspective of him. How am I supposed to leave now, Watch? Is this how it ends? No matter what... he wins. Does he think the more I know the easier it will be to get me to stay...? another trap to keep me inside the fortress we call home? He's going to have to learn that the world is not full of Spikes waiting to hurt him. He's allowing old events to shape his tomorrows. This world has changed. I have to be free from this house. This godforsaken Orchard. He's going to have to understand. His personal prison is worse than the places jailers put him in. This world does not revolve around him and his experiences. He is still the same person as yesterday. The story doesn't change the fact that mama died alone. In fact, it only makes it worse. He knows what it's like to be in prison. He knows what it is like not to be free and still he chains his family to a place we can't leave. Holding me down with shackles of guilt that bond me to this land. This story is just his way of forming another iron grip to hold and anchor me. Why? So, he can see me die like he did mama and that old jeweler. This story won't end with me dying in front of him. I won't let him stand there while I take my last breath.

BETWEEN HOPE AND LIBERTY

Justus

This bird looks over me while I lie in bed. Why did I have Dr. Keeler Move his cage in here? His right eye fixed on me. Is it possible to feel guilt from the eyes of a parrot? Dr. Keeler left over two hours ago. Faith has been gone over an hour on a twenty-minute round trip drive to the store. She only went to get the medication for my pain prescription. My hip isn't broken.... My leg is ok. Bed rest for three or four weeks with this bird watching me. It's clear my revelations about the past have served my Faith as a stressful burden of knowledge. My old friend the doctor expressed sadness while talking about Hope. I wish he could cure my real problem.

"Squawk... Swooos!"

I hear her car when it pulls to a stop. The engine shuts off. She waits until finally, I hear the car door open. It closes. Then her steps on the porch. Watch's steps scratching against the wood on the porch. His tail wagging. I hear it slap against the banister posts on the porch. Her keys enter the lock of the door. The door opens. My pulse reacts and quickens as though I was going outside. She closes the door gently. Watch's tail still thumping against the walls.

"Squawk! Swoos… Squawk! Swooos!"

Shhh did his little dance he bobbed his head and lifted one of his claws. He flapped his wings and turned his body around to face the window. Faith entered the room.

"Dad, how do you feel? Dr. Keeler called me on his way out."

My heart still raced.

"Faith honey…can you get my bottle from the living room?"

She left the room without saying a word. I wished Hope was here. She could've helped me tell the rest of this story. I had to do this right. I contemplated my next course of action. My thoughts and feelings based on a nightmare of confusion. The rough streets I come from are far from my Faith's rationale. Can Faith grasp the concept of what it takes to live life in the streets of the city?

No matter how much I hate it, for Faith's sake I've got to finish reliving this story.

"Here, dad… do you want… are you ok?"

Her eyes didn't meet mine. She pushed her hand through her luxurious hair.

"Yes, baby girl I'm okay. "

Shhh looked over his shoulder. I summoned the courage.

"Sweetheart… I need to finish this story. It won't take too much of your time. "

She looked at me and then looked away to the floor.

"I'll stay for a minute, but I have to go, dad. I can't stay."

"Thank you. "

"You don't have to thank me, dad."

She pushed her hand through her hair again.

"Honey… is there anything you want to ask me?"

She looked away. A vision of her mother ... My baby girl had grown into such a beautiful woman.

"No, dad, I'm, well, it's all so much to take in. You had this whole other life and I still don't' know how you met mama. You haven't mentioned her once. "Did you ever love mama? Did you ever love her? Did you? Daddy, she's dead and the only part of your story I've heard up till now doesn't even involve her. When you said there was something you wanted to tell me I thought maybe it might be about her…it wasn't. It was just about you again. What about her? Daddy, did you love her? Did you?"

"Faith yes! I loved Hope with all my heart. She was my wife. The reason why I didn't show it properly is what I'm trying to explain to you. We were ripped from all we know to live here. Chains kept us apart and chains kept us together. Do you remember her eyes Faith? Do you remember your mother's eyes?"

My teary-eyed princess. She'd been stroking her hair for years trying to figure out a way to say that. From my Faith's mouth came an agonizing cry that vibrated into me with open arms. My baby came into my embrace. She held me so tight. We melted into the moment. The cry she'd been holding in most of her life finally came out. Shhhh turned around slightly to look upon us in his left eye. He flapped his wings without uttering a sound from his beak. As usual, he recorded the moments of this house and this family with a watchful eye. The strength of her cries lessened. The strength of my arms eased her from my chest. As she lifted away the separation felt magnetized. Not so much a force of her being drawn back down but more the draw of her energy pulling me upwards.

"Do you remember her eyes Faith?"

"Yes… yes, daddy. I can remember her eyes. They were beautiful." She eased a spot on the edge of my bed. I scooted back to give her more room.

"Her eyes were the first thing that caught my attention. Do you have a cigarette?"

She reached into her pocket, retrieved the pack and tapped out a smoke for me and one for her.

"Her eyes were like pools of water… ahh... yeah, your mom's eyes reflected the sky during a warm sunny day with no clouds"

Faith leaned back, positioning her body so she could lay her head on my chest looking up at the ceiling. I laid flat on my back to give her more comfort. She took puffs of smoke blowing them towards the foot of the bed.

"Your mother's eyes looked like heaven on earth. I was drawn to them. When she looked at me my control fell under a higher power. She changed the rhythm of my movement. Her eyes. Looking at her eyes just made sense.

Hope and I were connected beyond the moment of first sight in this life. She held me in a trance and I just moved towards her. The moment your mother's eyes gazed upon me, the messed-up prison world felt hopeful. I assumed My place and my purpose in that living nightmare. Hope's eyes…your mother's eyes…they revitalized me. After sitting in a cell spinning days and nights into months, I'd been released to my first physical day to day contact with a woman. Hope was a teacher at the prison."

Faith lifted her head and turned to look at me.

"Faith… your mother was my teacher and I remained her student from then on. In that moment I didn't know she'd be my wife. I didn't know she'd be your mother. But that moment of first-sight still remains in my heart."

Shhh turned to face us, Watch came into the room. The smoke exited my lungs. "Squawk Never believe love's a fantasy. Squawk! Swooos. Believe in love."

"Dad, you have a really crazy bird."

My baby smiled. "We have a crazy bird Faith. He's part of our family."

Shhh did his dance and turned around to face the land.

"Prison is no easy place. Being in prison removes rights and privileges most of us take for granted. Your mother's heart was as light as a feather. Hope didn't see all the corruption and lawless ways of the people in a place where most say making a difference doesn't matter. The Bible and all the holy books only assign saving souls to saints and angels. Your mother … Hope was an angel in a very dark place. Men far worse than my old friend Spike sat in her presence learning how to be better men than what they knew and what they were before. Imagine how difficult it must be to devote your time and energy to people who feel life isn't worth much more than nothing. What of life is left to save from that? Why care about the condemn of society, some are sentenced to die in captivity. Who cares about a person sentenced to life in prison? If that person dies who outside their family gives it much thought? A person unjustly killed in our streets has strangers who care and rally support to help mourning family members no matter what they have done or what they were involved in. What happens to innocent citizens in prison who are killed after wrongfully losing their life of freedom? Her eyes were the first thing I saw. They drew me near and pulled me in. She held her own as firm and no-nonsense. Hardened criminals were going to learn from her or else they could leave. She had no problem sending anyone who didn't want to learn out of the class in exchange for someone who did. Most of the guys in class came to get away from the daily madness of prison life. Hope gave us sanctuary to enjoy peace, growth, and education. I'm a cynical person by nature. Who was this woman I thought? I was raised in the city where things were not always as they seemed. I don't think I ever met a person in the city who wasn't out for something. Everybody had an angle for what they wanted in the city. Your mother was a teacher who got paid for her work. She wasn't a volunteer. Yeah, she had pretty eyes but what did that mean? The job didn't pay much but there was always some Spoiled rich girl who wanted to prove her value to other rich people by taking a job that showed disdain for money and standards. There's more than one way to get paid out of life. Money isn't the only thing that pays people with satisfaction. I know people with money who hate themselves and thrive off sadistic pleasures. They use others less important to make themselves feel better. After my initial draw to Hope I put up walls of protection. I figured she was using us and this job to make herself feel better. We didn't matter. Any criminal or convict could be sitting in her classroom seats. Yeah, she had pretty eyes, but she wasn't going to fool me. Other guys would try to flirt with her and create fantasies of a more personal relationship between them. Not me. I came for the sanctuary and growth. It cost me money out of my monthly canteen draw to get in the class. That's how prison works. Everything had a price, and nothing came free. Even with old friends you knew before being in prison together you couldn't freeload. If you didn't contribute, you'd fall to the bottom of the food chain quick. I paid half my monthly food draw to get in that class. I didn't have a prison hustle. I didn't know how to draw, cook, fix, or make anything. I refuse to sell drugs. I thought about working in the kitchen washing dishes. The kitchen was a place where food was cooked. Making twenty egg, ham and cheese sandwiches a day could turn into a few hundred dollars a month. The only thing I knew how to do up to that point was rob, wash dishes, and sweep floors. The only money I had in prison was from Liberty and it wasn't much. Your grandmother didn't really have much extra income after her bar money and bills. She did what she could. I wasn't rich, or high on the totem pole in prison society. Most guys with my bid of life without the possibility of parole would have wanted to work in the kitchen to have free food and a prison hustle. The odds were stacked against me trying to survive without a hustle in prison. Older guys who'd been down twenty years or better had stories of women they no longer held contact with. Those sad stories would always grip me with fear. My stomach would twist with butterflies, my heart would pound as I listened to their stories. Losing my Liberty would surely kill me. My Liberty, Faith, was all I had left. I didn't have an innocent belief about myself as to why I was in prison. To endure the harshness of my sentence I had to accept what I had done in my part of the crime. I went to rob the jewelry store owner. I wasn't completely innocent in his death. I had done my part. There was no pity party for me; I paid to get into Hope's class with half my monthly food supply so I could turn my negative situation into a positive one. I figured if Liberty left me I would at least enjoy my time with her and not worry about life without her. Why miss a moment together worrying about spending moments apart? The clock always ticks toward something. The woman…the teacher with the pretty eyes had her angle and I had mine. I want to say it was love at first sight but I'm not sure if that is what it was. Looking back, I think I just… we just recognized each other and connected. She said she'd noticed me. I know I noticed her."

"Daddy?"

That word reminded me of old times telling her stories before bed.

"Yes Faith"

She moved her head up higher on my chest and took the burning cigarette butt out of my hand.

"How did you and mama first kiss?"

My heart beat a bit out of rhythm. I wondered if Faith could feel it. What's in a kiss? When I kissed Hope, it wasn't magical, but I couldn't tell Faith that. How could I put it? Shhh flapped his wings.

"Have you ever had a friend who you love in a way that is more than friendly but sex or physical attraction is out of the question?"

"Yeah, me and Rob started out like that. We were friends first. Dad, I want you to meet him" Faith beamed a radiant aura of light like a newly born star from the center of darkness.

"One day he and I will meet."

"Can it be someday soon, daddy?"

I paused. This moment a dream come true. My Faith sought my approval. "Yes, it can be soon. I'd like to meet the man who holds the meaning of my Faith's heart."

"I'd like that very much dad, thank you."

I squeezed her tight in my right arm.

"It's important Faith; I'm sorry it took this long." Shhh... flapped his wings still looking out at the land. I continued.

"Your mother and I didn't start off as friends or lovers. She was my teacher. I was her student. Sex and lust weren't a consideration or even in the realm of options for us. The classroom our sanctuary the only place for both of us to have peace. Your mother was with a very abusive man when I met her. Her husband treated her with coldness. The first time I noticed her eyes red and puffy I didn't know what to say. So, I stayed away. The second time I noticed I stayed in her presence all day talking about life, Religion, politics, relationships, philosophy, education. She knew how to provoke profound thoughts in a subtle way without much controversy. That first conversation led to so many more. I'd think about things she said and things we talked about late at night in my cell. She'd later tell me she did the same thing at her home. There wasn't a sexual attraction, but one day I'd had enough of watching her hurt, and I told her that and the full story came out ... that's when we kissed. No plan or intended purpose. Time passed between us and then it happened.

"What happened after the kiss daddy? Did you fall in love with mama then? "

I wanted to sip from the bottle of spirits but to do so would move my Faith.

"Squawk! Squawk!"

Shhh. flapped his wings. His back still to us. I continued.

"After the first kiss, we backed away quickly. We were afraid of physical contact. We could've gotten into a lot of trouble for just touching each other. The kiss would have made so much of a serious situation that Hope would have lost her job and I'd have been sent to another prison far away, so as soon as it was over we both acted like it didn't happen. But I thought about her all night.

"Not all of it was good Faith. I'd cheated on my Liberty with Hope. Kissing another woman during my stay in prison when she wouldn't dare touch another man in the city streets was a sin against our love. I'd allowed the teacher with the beautiful eyes to draw me in and now I'd cheated on my love. I didn't go to class the day after that kiss... two days... three days I still hadn't gone back. The weekend came four days after and as usual, my Liberty was there to visit me. Even though it wasn't a surprise I felt startled when they called my name to visit.

Being selfish is when you cheat on love Faith. Cheating is no better than stealing. I'd stolen something from Liberty and I didn't know if my selfishness could be forgiven. I didn't want to bring any more pain. Confessing to her felt...wrong. It didn't feel worth the price, to be honest. There... It wasn't an affair. It was a kiss. Telling her meant hurting her for what reason, other than my conscious about cheating. Someday I'd have to confess but that day I didn't. Physical contact at the prison: the beginning and ending of a visit you are allowed a brief hug and kiss. She had something she wanted to ask me. Being so caught up with my issues of selfishness I had a hard time paying attention for most of that visit. She held her usual excitement. Liberty's words flowed into my ears in their usual hypnotizing melody. Her voice hummed a tune I never grew tired of. Background music that etched into my memories. I really couldn't focus on deciphering her words that day. My senses were overloaded when she said, 'I want to have a baby with you.' Out of my head and back to the visiting room. Having a child is something I'd never thought of until that moment in my life. The first time my mind conceived something that beautiful was just days after I'd committed a terrible act against my love. My pulse raced. My nerves twisted. My temperature rose. I began to perspire. To say our conversation about creating a child in prison went magically would be a lie. I almost passed out, but eventually, I was able to fully mask again. She had to know something wasn't right during our conversation. Liberty always knew when something wasn't right. I went back to my cell after our visit and felt even worse about cheating. I laid in bed that night listening to our favorite songs in my headphones trying to make sense of what I'd done.

That Monday came fast. Playing back my memories I don't remember what I did between the visit and the Monday morning before school, but a whole day passed between those two events and it only feels like the blink of a moment. My nerves were on edge that morning. What if Hope got scared and told the guards I'd forced myself on her? Liberty would find out and our relationship would be over. I would lose my sanctuary and my Liberty all at once. As I made my way to the class that morning, I felt like everyone knew. Justus the fool of the moment paraded past all the onlookers of judgment. My shame beat my heart against my chest like the final gavel of conviction. My anxiety controlled the minutes, as I thought soon everything would be over.

I crossed the threshold into Hope's class. Only a few other students were present when I entered. Maybe she hadn't told anyone. Hope looked up at me from her desk and then she looked back down. The small room she sat in had a larger window looking out into the classroom. She could see everyone walking in. Her desk faced the double pane security window which looked from her office to the class. A panic room for safety when things went wrong. My mind felt relief when it became clear that the authorities did not know. I didn't want to go to a darker part of the prison system. She later told me all those days I was absent from class she restlessly waited for my return. Hope thought I wasn't coming back. That day after class she called me into her office and told me that kiss was a mistake and it shouldn't happen again. We both understood the boundaries which held us apart and the thin threads of circumstance which held us together but still, we became closer than before. I was beginning to fall in love with her...Faith do you mind grabbing me something to eat from the kitchen? Maybe some peanut butter and bread. I can make it into a sandwich myself. I just need to put something on my stomach. This medicine is strong."

She got up.

"Sure Dad, I'll cook you something. Is there anything special you'd like?

"No honey… Nothing special. Whatever you think is best. Not too big a fuss ok."

She ran her fingers through her hair.

"Dad?"

Already up I took a few sips from my spirits.

"Yes, Faith."

"Thank you for telling me about you and mama's first kiss. I'd always wanted to know.

"You're welcome, honey."

She ran her fingers through her hair again.

"Can you tell me more after we eat?"

"Of course, Faith. Anything for you. I love you."

"I love you too, dad."

JUSTICE DREAMS OF HOPE

Hope inside Justus' dream

From my station of life's perspective, I'm shaken imprisoned under the conditions of my position. What life have I seen outside exposure? I only know what I know. Here's the problem: Justus! Faith! Faith! Justus! They don't get close enough to truly know one another. How do I bring Justus and Faith together without holding court over a world of trouble? A nation reduced to rubble civilization builds a home upon. It's more than bricks and stones or concrete foundations laid into the ground. Work, more work through the birth of new moments. I worry that I'm burying my deliverance at the same time I receive it. I trust this world might someday grant me forgiveness for my imperfection, but only suggestions come to answer my requests for direction in guiding my lessons of reflection. A meaningful message measures the length of a sentence. Order in the court of public opinion. Shhhh. Watch. I was born into this place to live off the land. I demand life with the sureness of death. Stolen moments of a life for satisfaction should be a sin. Is it? In love with a conflict. My Faith and my Justus refuse to see each other and both point the finger of imperfection without having any faults. I plead with Faith when we talk, but during the dispute, she expresses no acknowledgement of previous wrongs. She constantly rewrites the meaning of what has happened and defines the moment with what's to come. We can only wait for Faith's interpretation of the future while she disregards the past with a warped sense of the present. Faith will force a circle shaped object into a square-shaped space because she believes she's right. How many of us practice in the way of Faith? Whoever believes their actions are that of perfection shall happily live in error as a fool who denies the truth. My Faith shares this world with Justus and tries to fight the reality of being in this house. That under which my Faith has lived is something that might as well have happened to someone else. Justus a product of society seeks to fit the model of right and wrong. My Justus wishes to go past man's law and natures law to find a law that Faith can understand. He lives as a right and not a privilege. When he's called to answer he responds like a witness. He holds his righteousness in sentence. He holds his misery in execution. Blindingly weighing the facts hand in hand. His past recollection. His future exists only to sustain him and yet he wishes he didn't have to be overruled in judgement on his appeal. Blind to love. Blind to compassion. He only sees the facts and that is why he can't see his own Faith.

In Judgement: What Do You Know?

Faith

My mother and father met in prison. I always thought they'd met in the city. I guess I just assumed they'd met in the city from listening to daddy's bedtime stories. Mama never really told stories. How they met was a mystery. I always wanted to know. The few times I asked Mama just changed the subject or gave a directive to do an undone chore. She had her ways of disregarding questions she didn't want answered. Eventually, I gave up trying to find out. Really until today, it had been a while since I cared. Don't really remember when I'd stopped caring about mama and daddy's relationship. As a little girl and still to this day I can't remember them showing much affection beyond daddy holding mama when she cried. Dinners were always quiet. When things were good, and mama was happy, she made daddy's favorite pork chops, green peas, butter and rice. She'd glow with pride as she cooked it and the house would smell so good. Stop all that yapping Watch! You know I'm cutting some fat off these pork chops for you? Just like mama used to do. I wonder how we got to this orchard. I can't wait to hear more from daddy over dinner. It's funny how when you aren't looking for something you always seem to find it. Today I woke up not really wanting to be here and really not wanting to talk to daddy. Now I'm cooking and hurrying to get back to hear more of this story. How do people live in the same house for years on top of years and know nothing about each other? Children lying to parents about who they are and what they really do in their private lives. Parents shielding their children from the truth about who they are as adults. Is anybody completely honest? I always thought my parents didn't understand me, but really, we didn't understand each other. How many of us live with people we think we know and yet in our understanding of misunderstanding we dislike some of their ways? There's danger in thinking we know all there is to know. The danger of not understanding exists in our interaction. I was interacting with mama thinking I knew her, and I really didn't know her at all. I stop listening to daddy because I thought…I thought…that's the problem, too much thought and not enough listening. Hmmm…. These pork chops smell good. Daddy's going to love it. I didn't foresee cooking dinner tonight. Heck, I didn't know I'd leave him lying back there in his bed with a bruised hip. Are we in control of our lives Watch? It seems to me like we fill in spaces for parts of a play we didn't write. I swear no matter how much I plan I never end up in the situation I planned for.

There was this birthday party I planned while living in the city going to college. It was for this girl named Cada Dia. She was hard to plan for because she was always so busy. City people are always busy doing things that matter or doing things that don't. Pinning her down long enough to commit to just a few hours wasn't easy. It was a surprise party. The girls in the dorm were all in on it. I planned the night to take place at a new hot wing sports bar. Cada Dia loved hot wing sports bars. Everything was perfect. All our friends from school were going to be there. I'd even went online and found her brother. His name was Sin Voz. Everything was set. The perfect plan. When Cada Dia walked through the door everybody yelled 'Surprise!' Even the waitress, hostesses and cashier chimed in. The happy birthday banner dropped down and she was shocked. Her mouth was wide open as her brother walked towards her smiling. Sin Voz had his arms opened. I was so happy. Everything was going according to my plan. Cada Dia ran out of the restaurant. We all stood a second of shock without talking and then gave chase. I caught up to her quickly. She'd stopped at a street-light crying. I wrapped my arms around Cada when I caught her. The others were coming but I yelled at them to go back. They hesitated; looking at me holding her. I screamed, "She doesn't need a crowd, go back!" Some hesitation remained but they went back. Cada Dia cried "who invited him?" I was afraid to tell her. I'd planned the whole thing. I asked her why she didn't want him there. She stopped crying and a look I'd never seen before came across her face. In a whisper, she said "He killed our father during a hunting trip and destroyed our family. I hate him, and I want him gone."

Everything made sense after that. When I'd talked to Sin Voz to invite him, he asked: "Are you sure you she wants me there?" In my naive raised-on-an-orchard-farm way I figured, of course, she'd want her brother to come. The problem. I assumed I knew her life. We'd been going to school together and living in the same dorm for two years but really what did I know about her beyond that? I apologized for inviting her brother and told Cada Dia I'd take her home. She didn't want to go home. She wanted to go back to the party and told me to make him leave. Before we went back she made me promise not to say anything about it. I promised and until now I never told anybody. Not even mama. You keep quiet Watch. Here's some fat for you. We went back to the party and her brother was gone. Cada was the consummate actress telling everybody she was just overwhelmed and had never had a gesture this grand done for her before. She then asked what happened to her brother. The others told us he'd left while we were gone. Cada said she'd call him, and he was used to her melodramatic behavior. A few girls asked me what really happened. I told them nothing and that was that.

I'd planned the perfect moment and, in my mind, nothing could go wrong. I thought I knew everything about my friend but when I thought about it, I hadn't asked her about her family life. I just assumed. We think we know the people in our lives – our friends, our family, our neighbors. Still. The people we hold dear can be complete strangers that we make into our own concepts of who they should be. So, are our friends and family the people we think they are or are they the people we think they should be? I have been disappointed over and over by people who do things I don't think they should do. My expectations of them are based on my beliefs about who they should be. When they show me who they are contrary to my expected assumptions I'm in shock. Why? Why should I be shocked when a person shows me who they are? I can't tell you how many times I've said. "I can't believe things about this or that person." People don't just tell other people all the truths about themselves. We all have things we'd rather not share and maybe it's not so much a secret rather than something we'd just like to keep private. For years I had to keep the secret of my life on this orchard. I have told people all sorts of things to keep this life private. In my foolish mind, I'd believed that other people's family lives were better than mine. Mama always used to say, "I know you hate it here but it's not the worst place on earth. You have a clean home with a mother and father who love you. Some people wish all their lives for a place like this. Always remember to be thankful for things you have instead of comparing them to things you don't." Stop all that barking Watch! Mama's words always get you stirred up. Yeah, she was right almost all the time. I can't think of too many times she was wrong. Being her daughter, I wished some of her wisdom would pass down to me but based on today I have a long way to go before that happens. How could I think my friend Cada's family life or anyone's family life didn't hold secrets just like mine? Every family has things they keep from outsiders. So, if we all keep secrets then we must be strangers because holding back key information for people to process who we are, denies the full content of our character. Do the people in our lives always know the true motives of why do we do what we do? We carry our behavior from birth to the next experience. That's with us wherever we go. There's an old saying that all people have skeletons in the closet. Who doesn't have skeletons hiding in their lives? We are skeletons in closets of flesh, moving on the individual choices from environmental reactions. I'm reasoning under impressions reflected in the world of my ego's existence. We show our most favorable selves and even vulnerability is subject to a little modification when openly expressed. Protective walls. Does this mean we are not honest with our peers, our family, our co-workers, our neighbors when we hide our weaknesses or our fears? The skeleton can't protect the spirit without the walls of flesh. Don't we have a right to privacy? If we do have a right to privacy, then why do some of us feel others are hiding things and shame them with guilt for keeping privacy in their lives?

At first, I was mad at daddy for keeping all these things from me. I drove to the store upset. I came back from holding my resentment worn down by my anger and in my fatigue, I was able to receive the message he was sharing his privacy with me. I think my awareness has won out over my anger and a type of honor has come over me. I have started to understand what he went through. I don't think we should feel guilty for having privacy or feel forced to share it. If people don't fully understand us then maybe it's because they're not supposed to.

When we view other people's lives does what see present the full picture? In the city, I constantly found people inserting themselves into other people's shoes. They'd look at someone and say "I'd never do that… I'd do this…" I had a college roommate who constantly on every subject and every topic talked about how she would have handled a situation in theory. Even television programs weren't safe. She'd watch a talk show and talk over the show about what she would have done in the situation. Well, one time she talked about what she would do if her boyfriend cheated on her. She said she'd play it cool and dump him. She wouldn't make a scene like the girls on TV. Wouldn't you know it, her boyfriend cheated on her and she made the biggest scene I've ever seen. Slapping and hitting him in the face. All of this happened on the open grass with a large crowd of onlookers at the grand entrance to the school. People intervened after she started slapping and hitting him. Once they pulled her off him, he screamed: "It's over!" Then turned his back and walked away. When he turned his back, she went crazy crying and screaming, "I love you, please don't leave" It was a really sad sight. Back then I was shocked by her actions. Based on what she said I really believed she was going to play it cool. I don't really put too much stock into what people say they are going to do anymore. Most of the time it's just tough talk with no real substance. I found more than just my old roommate said things to do and when the time came didn't do them. If we can't trust what people tell us all the time, then what can we assume we know about them?

Rob is my joy and my salvation, yet he doesn't know all about me. I didn't… I don't tell him about my fights with dad. Rob assumes all is well between me and Daddy. I see now it's my fault and I owe him the truth about this situation. He deserves to know. Come on Watch. Daddy's dinner is done. Let's take it to him.

BETWEEN LIBERTY AND HOPE

Justus

"Squawk! The answers are from questions. Squawk! Answers from questions. Swoos." Awoken by those words. Hope's words. A phrase from my beloved throated through his beak. How I miss her. When I dream about her my fear is to wake up. I'm convicted to regret, and Regret holds no peace. You can't change the past ...the past gives us an identity. For some, the past controls the future, and fear stands them still in the existing moment. Who doesn't have at least a wish to change one thing that happened in their lives? Some say they live life with no regret but if they could change at least one thing in their past would they refuse? Maybe the lesser degrees of regret can cause people to believe they don't have events they wish they could go back and change. The ability to embrace regret might be the reason those people feel they don't have any. Embracing regret doesn't mean you only have experiences of perfection. If you say there's nothing in your life you wish had been different then you are a pompous perfect and we all need to learn your secret to having the ideal life without error. Hmm... Something smells good.

"Squawk! Swoos." my Faith walked in holding a heavenly meal. The faint smile on her face grew with the look of surprise that appeared on mine. She resembled so much of her mother. Faith carrying this familiar plate of food brought back flashes of my beautiful Hope. I closed my eyes and prayed for forgiveness.

"Thank you, Faith."

"It's ok, dad, you don't have to thank me it's my pleasure. Eat your supper."

I sat the plate on my lap grabbed the knife and fork and carved up the delicious chop of meat before me. Eager to take a bite. The taste... Just like her mother used to make. Shhh did his little dance while looking at me with his right eye. He lifted one claw up and put it down then lifted his other claw and put it down. I took another bite of food. Anticipating his squawk, I chewed the succulent piece of meat my eyes closed savoring the flavor. Hope's recipe, I'm back to the moment. My Faith smiled. Shhh's back to us again.

"This is the first meal your mother ever cooked for me, pork chops, green peas, butter and rice. She snuck it into work as a treat, and what a treat it was. Delicious home cooking from the hands of a beautiful woman with pretty eyes. I had to eat it fast. She watched me devour the sustenance with a beaming glow. I don't know what draws two people together. What makes love? A wish to be with someone? I suppose if we didn't wish for companions there wouldn't be societies and civilizations, but that's not love."

Faith smiled at my humor sitting on the edge of the bed with her plate. Old memories of days gone by circulated in my mind Shhh fluttered a little, still facing the land.

"Hope and I held love between us like a sacred flame, but it was a forbidden blaze under extreme conditions. A solid bond formed between us through shared desires. What lay outside our love could not come between us. We were one in fighting the extreme conditions of exposure. Our sacred flame. Everything against us only made us grow closer. What ignited us, what burned between us removed and consumed the obstacles around us. Until that day I'd never had a home-cooked dream of tastes especially prepared for me. I was raised on frozen TV dinners and processed take out. Honestly, I'd never eaten a piece of meat so sweet until I found Hope. She told me about her famous chops in our prison talks. Her ex-husband didn't like them. The first time he tasted them he complained and told her never again would he eat something like that. I couldn't believe how mean and selfish he was to a woman who loved, honored, and obeyed him. It wasn't that he didn't like fat juicy chops. He just criticized everything she did. He'd berate her for nothing and it seemed nothing from her made him happy. Faith, I know from the outside looking in I didn't show great affection towards Hope but through our unique bond, our unique connection I made sure she knew her love saved me. I never talked down to her. She found ways to make me happy every day; and although Your miserable father held loss and misery as a delusional shield to cover up my spoiled heart, I know…I know how lucky… I was. This beautiful woman with sparkling eyes loved me beyond death and not many men imprisoned or free could lay stake to a claim like that. As your mother and I grew closer under the wielding forces bonding our reasons for being together, Liberty and I grew further apart. We worked on our conception. I would smuggle my essence for our seed in a balloon wrapped tight. I'd place the essence in my mouth under my tongue and during our brief kiss, I'd give her the prospect of our dreams. She'd take it to the women's restroom place it inside her and return to hold my hand for as long as could be without letting go. All we wanted was to have our wish come true. Our dream. At times, I grew confused. What was I doing? I felt like I'd lost my mind. I was ashamed for loving both women at the same time. What kind of a man was I to cheat on the first woman to love me as her husband? My heart ached to have Liberty. We were together in holy matrimony. Wedlocked in court after my sentencing. The affair with Hope meant being unfaithful to my wife."

I took a bite of food, but the meat no longer tasted the same. The chew produced warm slimy squirts of juice under the force of my jaws. I did my best to cover up the sour taste exploding inside my mouth.

"I cheated on Liberty to be with Hope and developed excuses based on justifications that didn't make sense. What could I tell myself to inspire a delusion that justified adultery against a union of trust? No matter what I came up with nothing satisfied my attempt to nourish this hungry salvation. Every attempt only feeding the verdict for my conviction of guilt. Selfish needs turn to regret in the hands of time. My account of failed attempts added up daily. I didn't want my love to turn into hate but the factors in my decision clouded my reasoning. Insanity in my efforts to change. My will wasn't strong enough to withstand my weaknesses. I couldn't tell myself a thing to ease the pain of remorse and regret. It hurt every time I looked into Liberty's eyes. She loved who I was, but she'd hate who I am."

"Squawk. Swoos."

Letting loose a few feathers Shhh interrupted us. His back was still to the room. I took another bite of sustenance. The punishing taste of bitterness took away my appetite. I sat the sacrificial offering of chopped animal flesh, grains and vegetables on the nightstand next to my spirits. Faith looking down now shuffled her fork around the food on her plate. Watch entered back into the room as if called by the energy of Faith's deliberations. We both knew what was coming next. She tore off a bite from the plate as Watch slowly moved towards her, lightly wagging his rear across the journey for her scraps. Faith gave Watch the offering from her hand. The sharp jaws gently grip the provision from her fingers. The rich treat secured by his teeth for a taste he moved away from Faith's delicate hands. Once out of reach he chewed with the fierce power of his greed swallowing away his earnings within the blink of an eye. In one motion, he finished with the licking of his teeth. Doing his ritual, he moved back towards Faith for another scrap. She already had one available. Shhh... flapped again letting loose a feather or two. This ending with a stretch of his wings for what I see as his imagination of being free, outside the cage. I continued.

"The full truth… Liberty had to know. I needed to solve the conflict within myself by letting it out. Our next visit I told Liberty what I'd been hiding. After I said "kissed" ... the words to my love put her face down in her hands. I had to stop I said, "I'm sorry." She looked up at me and said, "I know" I moved my eyes to avoid hers. My shame and the strength in my muscles became one. My only choice to trade places and look down into my lap. She said it again in tone fierce with damnation. "I KNOW! I know you're sorry." She said. She told me she knew I was doing something against us for some time and she prayed for it to stop. She stood up from her seat. Tears running from her eyes she cried. "I knew your love was a lie." The price of freedom. Liberty walked out of my life. I'd never see her again."

I'd never told another person this testimony. Shhh had listened to it countless times. He flapped once more and turned around from the land to face us. Faith sat her plate of food on the floor. Watch moved in to claim the prize. I reached for a taste of the spirits.

"I never told Hope what happened between Liberty and I and we never spoke of Liberty again but after our breakup, nothing brought me comfort. I was in pieces. No more visits. No more perfumed letters. No more calls home. What remained in Liberty's place was a void where she'd once been. The moments without her turned into the torturous reminders of what we once shared. Hearing the other men's names called for visits became the calls of what I'd lost. Each time the loudspeaker sounded I wished it was me going to see her. A few times I thought they'd called me. They hadn't. I wrote letters to Liberty every day but they went unanswered. I'd stand at the door during mail call waiting for the officers to stop at my cell. For weeks and weeks, the officers just walked by with no hesitation. Then one day an officer stopped and called my name. "Justus!" My heart skipped a beat. I'd all but given up. He handed me three letters, the breath left my body. The officer's head shook back and forth as if to pity me. While I looked down at the mail in my hand the officer walked off. I recognized the writing on the envelope. The familiar writing covered by an unfamiliar stamp from the post office. 'Return to sender'. My heart sank to the bottom of my stomach. My Liberty was really gone."

I took a deep swallow of my homemade spirits and tried to lessen some of the pain from reliving this story out loud. Shhhh looked at me with his left eye now. Watch with a full belly of pork laid stretched out on the floor. Faith lit a smoke. I continued.

"We never know how much we miss something until it's gone. Even the small things we do every day can have a big impact when taken away. Prison took away many of the freedoms I took for granted. The ability to talk with loved ones when they called or just take a walk at night under the stars were things I could no longer do even with privilege or permission. In some strange way, I thought I'd lost all I could lose. I sat with those three letters and cried under my breath. It took a while for me to calm down from the rejection, but it finally came to my thoughts as a math equation. 'I'd written more than twenty letters, and only three had been returned.' Those were the last three I'd written so she had to have received the other 17. A smile came over me. I gripped the returned letters tight and felt my Liberty had sent me a message to stop pleading and give her time to think and respond. Somehow, I found comfort that someday Liberty would return. That's the thing about prison. Delusions of optimism are sometimes the only things which can sustain the convict's sanity. My belief that Liberty would return gave me the strength I needed to face that she was gone. The appeal in my court case gave me the solace I needed to face my conviction. Holding those returned letters in that moment of delusion made it seem that love was not lost but as you can see, Liberty never returned. She didn't send me another letter. For many weeks and months, I believed she would. That false sense wrapped me up like a blanket and I held that blanket more than the blanket held me because I needed it. That's the good thing about delusions. They help quiet the painful memories of regret. I have not forgotten about Liberty and when times are quiet her image returns to me. My mind still seeks ways to rationalize not seeing her again. Drinking helped me find the perceptions I needed for temporary relief from guilt. The guilty feelings of conviction. I'd give anything to see Liberty again. When I think of the day she left me I just wish that she'd turn around. The only thing I've wished for is another chance to see her. A wish that I know will never come to be. It's taken me years to accept she's not coming back and what I regret most, Faith.

"The thing I most regret about that day is that I didn't hold her longer when we first embraced. I wish I could have held her just a little bit more. Your mother made this meal for me whenever she felt I needed something to feel free but my love for her held a secret: I stopped sharing her enthusiasm for this meal once we moved here. She'd make it and I'd feel regret with each bite. This meal represented all that I had lost when Liberty left. Yes, I found the delusions to get me through the initial loss, but as the years went on the painful truth always found a way to squeeze past the illusions. Nothing can quiet and hide the truth inside forever. I'd cheated Liberty and betrayed our love and for that, I'd have to grin and enjoy every bite.

"Squawk!!"

Shhh wiggled and bobbed his head from side to side. Faith's eyes fixed on me, eager to dole out punishment.

"You never liked this meal?"

Her words cut through the air like a knife.

"No…that's not what I said Faith."

"That's exactly what you said."

"No honey that's not – "

"Don't call me that."

"Faith… Hon… calm down." She repeatedly ran her fingers through her hair. I could see the tears well in the corner of her eyes.

"Don't tell me to calm down. For years I watched mom make this meal for you and for years I watched you eat it. The entire time you didn't even like it?"

The pain in my hip crept through my intoxication I grabbed the pill bottle off the nightstand. "Faith, that's not what I mean. I loved your mother, that's why I ..."

"Liar! Squawk!"

Shhh interrupted us, flapping.

"Squawk! You're a liar! Sooos… You're a liar."

Faith laughed.

"You know what dad? That's the first time I ever cared to hear anything coming out of that bird's beak."

"Faith…"

She stood over me. Her arms folded.

"Don't, don't you dare. I want to know how we got here. Why did you and mom pick this place?"

I gripped the spirits. My plate of half-eaten meat and untouched peas and rice seemed to laugh at me. There was always something evil about this meal. I should have known when I saw the plate. Trouble was coming.

"Dad, I want to know. How did we get here?" I grip my bottle tighter and took another sip. "Ok honey, Ok. It's time for you to know about this land, and how we got here."

Shhh flapped his wings

"Squawk! Dinner is served… Squawk! Dinner is served. Swoos!"

THE SHADOWS OF CONFESSION
Faith

That house. The land, it must be cursed. When I was a little girl a ghost would come into my room. My dreams have always been filled with wonders and wishes but never with the truth. Looking out through my window at night under the moon, I'd see shadowy figures flying through the sky. The shadows of my fears moving at the speed of light traveling inside the darkness of the night. I'd stare for so long my eyes would get accustomed to the fear of watching them move. That's when they would slow down to a point where I could see their individualities. Their camouflage faces always smiling and laughing. Underneath the stars, these creatures would come out. As part of the background. Some would emerge from their graves oblivious to me, but others would come out fully aware that I could see and those are the ones who would come inside to be in the house with me. After years of watching shadows under the stars, I began to question why and who they are. Tonight had been another full of ghosts. The haunted land swarmed with shadowy figures as father's confession of how we got here made me cry. All those nights I spent looking outside I always wished he would come in and save me one time. He never did. The funny thing about fears is once you have encountered the conjured you move past them to form new boundaries between uncertain and reality. Tonight, as the shadows lifted out of their graves I found the answers written across their face.

He gripped his trusty spirits and told me the truth about him and his demons of regret and I'm surprised he didn't intoxicate himself to death. That stupid bird called him a liar. Maybe the bird and I have more in common than I thought. His Liberty. His beautiful Liberty. What about me and mama? He never liked the orchard and thought talking with watering eyes about a cursed heart to a half-opened mind would make everything alright. Shouldn't he thank his lucky stars mama got him out?

In prison, they used to talk about the land during their private times. Mama had grown up there. Her family owned it but she didn't want it. Mama had grown up working the orchard with her mother. She didn't know her father very well. A family trait I guess. When mama revealed her life to dad, he felt foolish for thinking the woman with the pretty eyes grew up as a rich girl. Mama's early life was spent gathering harvest with migrant workers like her mother. Dad had grown up with more luxuries than her. Mama started her life sleeping in a worker shed. My grandmother was an undocumented illegal worker who'd come here looking for a way to make a better life. Instead, she met a man who abused her and treated her like a tool for his pleasure. The story my mama told daddy about my grandmother was that my grandma had fallen in love with the land lord's son. From what she told dad it wasn't love at all. The lord's son would sneak her out to random places on the farm to have his pleasures with her. At the time, far away from home grandma believed that he loved her. She'd fought off all the advances of the older migrant workers only to let the owner's son overcome her defenses. Night after night he snuck her outside to have his way with her and day after day, he proudly walked past her as if she didn't exist. She was so young she didn't know she was pregnant with mama. She started showing. The son noticed one night and begged her not to tell. He didn't want the others to know what he had done. He stopped coming to see her at night and broke grandma's, young naive heart. Another girl was also pregnant, but she lost the child. The landlord saw the two young girls and wondered what was happening to their innocence. He felt sorry for them and demanded to know who was responsible for the abuses on his land. He thought one of the older workers had molested them. The owner was a good church person and did right where he could. Grandma didn't tell the owner and neither did the workers but when confronted the son admitted it. The owner called grandma into the main house and in front of his son, he told her he would help her. He sent his son away and told grandma the land was her home. That didn't mean she'd sleep in the house. No, she'd still work like everyone else, but he gave her a private shed with the other pregnant girl. Life wasn't easy after moving into that shed. Many of the other workers treated her coldly because she stood under the favor of the lord on his land. Late at night on Christmas Eve she gave birth to mama. The farm owner's wife helped deliver mama into the world. The owner's family had been holding hands in prayer over Christmas dinner when grand-mama had gone into labor. The owner's wife rushed out and found mama with an umbilical cord wrapped around her neck. A skilled woman at delivering newly born children the owner's wife saved my grandmother's life and delivered Hope unto the world. Mama never told me any of this. It must have hurt her bad. As an infant mama spent most of her day with the owner's wife while the others worked in the field. At eight years old mama began learning the ways of the land. She was homeschooled by the owner's wife who was also a retired elementary school teacher. This went on for some years then mama's life changed. At twelve years old grandma got sick. The illness didn't go away and within a year of contracting the disease, she passed. All mama had left were the landlords. The owner of the house wanted mama sent away to a convent, but the wife wouldn't have it. She moved mama into the main house and continued educating her about the world. Daddy couldn't recall if mama had ever told him the farm owner's name. He was certain she'd only called him the owner or him. Daddy did remember my great-grandmothers' name. The owner's wife, Irene. For the woman he described, her name was perfect. The Goddess of Peace. Mama had a similar life to mine. Homeschooled and trapped on an estate till she left for college. I find a sense of pride knowing mama grew up just like me. When mama's mama died her life changed unexpectedly. The echo: When my mama died my life changed unexpectedly. My grandfather didn't love my grandmother. The echo: My father didn't love my mother. My existence created from two people being together under circumstances that served their own purpose. Daddy was with my mama for opportunity and my mama was with daddy because of desperation. The echo: mama's mother and father found each other under similar circumstances. Listening to this story I'm not sure if mama's destiny isn't my own. From my grandfathers to my father and from my grandmothers to my mother it all seems to be one big string of misfortune where if one of my ancestors would've had a better opportunity I wouldn't be me, the miracle of reflection echoing their mistakes. I listened to his story getting madder and madder watching him drink his trusty spirits when I realize these occurrences weren't accidents at all. As a child, I felt alone in my life on this haunted land. After hearing mama's story, I don't feel so unique. My identity is important for being me but Still, the world doesn't stop when one person dies. There was this story of a woman who'd been kidnapped as a little girl and held for over 15 years by an evil man who raped her innocence daily. During her confinement, she became pregnant and gave birth to a child fathered by her rapist. At first, I thought how horrible for the woman to have given birth to her rapist's child but during the interview, the woman said, "The child was a part of her and being imprisoned with her child gave her something to love in the nightmare she lived being imprisoned by her rapist." We claim to be unique in our experience, but our experience isn't unique in relation to history. She wasn't the first woman to experience having her rapist's child. These things have happened to other women in past times. We are not all created by two people who love each other. And being created through love doesn't equal a more meaningful life. As a child lying in bed unable to sleep watching ghostly shadows fly and dance over me I used to ask myself, 'why was I created?'

This question held me in tears as a child and I found no answers until tonight. Just like the woman held captive by her rapist my mother loved me, and her mother loved her, and it didn't matter how we were created but It did matter why we were created. We were not made by love. We were made for love. No accident. Echoes of identity for the moment. Great-grandma Mrs Irene raised my mama and when mama went off to college, she hadn't been to a regular school growing up. College was a big adjustment for her. Like me, college was where mama experienced independence and first freedoms. A life in the city. Mama told daddy that Irene was so proud of her going to college that she promised not even death would keep her from being at mama's graduation. Mama would travel back at least once a month on a four-hour drive to spend a weekend with great-grandma Irene. A few years went on like this and then mama found her first love. Come on Watch you calm down. Good boy.

He was a frat jerk but mama being fresh off an orchard didn't know the difference between a jerk and a nice guy. His name was Samsara. I believe he loved mama at first. A home-schooled innocent young woman was a good catch for a city slick young man in college. Samsara never met Mrs Irene. Right before mama's graduation, she passed away. All the family mama had in this world after that was gone. The owner who mama never referred to as family gave her some money Mrs Irene had wanted her to have to finish college. He didn't come to mama's graduation. He rarely returned mama's calls and he never invited her back to visit. Nobody came to see mama graduate from college. All she had was the jerk she met, who would later become her husband at a city hall wedding.

From what daddy told me Mama and Samsara seemed happy with each other at first. He said Mama always believed there was a period in the beginning when she and he were happy. From daddy's perspective, Sam only used mama. Sam didn't finish college. Mama graduated and received her credentials. She always wanted to be a teacher. Samsara found temporary work at various jobs, but he had no career goals in mind. Relief from their stress came when mama got the job at the prison. She didn't take the job initially to help prisoners. She took the job because it paid good money that she and Sam needed. They moved near the prison and bought a small house. Looking for something to do Sam found a job as a used car salesman. It did more harm than good. His bad months of not selling cars were bad times for mama at home. As the bad months became more numerous at home mama found herself trying to avoid Samsara by being as quiet as possible. She tried to love and support him but slowly the bad time built up and mama ran out of things to say or do that could please him.

Daddy said the sound of her voice seemed to stir his anger and soon He began sleeping on the couch. Sometimes she'd wake up in the middle of the night to find him not on the couch and not in the house at all. Sometimes there would be days upon days where they'd barely speak a word to each other. Mama stopped sharing her day and her life with him. He never really shared much with her, to begin with. Mama lived with a strange wish that someday things would get better. She rationalized his behavior as a temporary phase of growing that would pass. She believed he had to love her or else he would have left. Why marry someone if you don't love them? Why stay in a relationship with someone you don't want to be with? In mama's mind there had to be some love for her in his heart. So, there was something to salvage. He always came home after being out with other women and mama felt the other women must be jealous of that.

Daddy said mama would smell their perfume on Sam's clothes and Some would seem to purposely leave lipstick marks on his collar or his neck. I know mama was sick inside knowing the man she married was giving himself to other women. Only finding comfort in thinking 'at least he comes home to me' but that didn't give her the satisfaction she really wanted. Mama tried to do things to make him notice her womanly appeal, but he never did notice. If he wanted to be with other women in his life, he should have left, but he tortured my mama's love by coming back. He barely touched her. When she tried to be seductive, he pushed her away. She faulted herself for putting on weight. She'd gained fifteen pounds. One day She got up early in the morning and started to exercise so she could lose weight. In two months she worked her way up to a two-mile run and 500 stomach crunches. She changed her diet and reached her goal. Mama lost 27 pounds in a few months, but Samsara didn't even notice. Quiet dinners and barely sleeping together continued. That's around the time she met daddy.

When we are hurting from a loss our vulnerable parts show in ways we may not be aware. So, we start looking for something similar to replace the thing we have lost. My mother and father were hurting from life's separation of attachments when they met. They both needed something more than what they had. On the quest to find synthetic parts for their missing pieces self-circumstance drew them to enjoy each other's wounds of insecurity. We gravitate towards things which make us happy. We look forward to our pleasures. Given a choice without pressure, we will move towards something we enjoy versus moving towards something we don't enjoy. This is our choice magnet in the instrumental compass of things that move us and dominate our daily activity. We are constantly looking for something to give us fulfillment and meaning. Daddy didn't want to spend his days wasting away in prison. He wanted freedom and in education, he found this satisfaction. Mama found herself in a place where she was grasping at straws in her attempt to find something to hold onto. Everywhere she turned stability eluded her. Her mama died. Her father she'd never known. Mrs Irene dies. Her husband barely acknowledges her without complaint. By process of elimination mama's job became the only thing she could call her own. Her work gave her fulfillment and purpose. Educating lost souls from darkness to enlightenment gave mama satisfaction. She didn't have to help the prisoners to receive her paycheck. The state didn't care about the education of lawbreakers. There wasn't a mandatory quota to reach. All that mattered to the state was that the class was filled with bodies. Mama could've sat and played on the computer all day and maybe if life with Samsara had been different, she would have. But mama went into work every day with a goal to educate and uplift souls that had been cast away. Then Daddy became something else for her to hold onto. Another source of pleasure for her gravitation.

I can't really understand why mama fell in love with someone like my daddy other than the desperation from loses. The usual things that bring two people together aren't always the same. Some see their mate without knowing love at first sight but eventually love does develop between them over time – so isn't that meeting love at first sight? What do you call it when two lives on a converging path of destiny meet and form a connection? Something about my daddy drew my mama to love him. From the story, daddy told tonight I can barely understand why any woman would want a man like him. From what he explained I don't really understand what he felt for mama. He talks about Liberty and I can see her love for him. He talks about mama's actions and I can see her love for him. He talks about his actions and all I can see is selfishness. My mama inherited the orchard from her father. He was never in her life as a nurturing parent raising a child to adulthood. They were just Two passing faces similar in nature but never one day acting in relation. Mama's father had been sent to a missionary church in another country. On his mission, her father worked with abused women who'd suffered horrible atrocities at the hands of men. From that experience, my mother's father devoted his life to church. He never married. Mama was his only known child. When he died, he left the orchard to mama but mama didn't want it. Samsara told her to sell it. Daddy told her not to and I know why. He had planned for his life of exile. Doing away with Samsara was the first step in his dreams of selfishness. I can't say he was wrong for getting rid of Samsara because I don't think Samsara really cared for mama, but I can say when you plan based on selfishness, you're manipulating the feelings of other people. Daddy paints a picture of a blossoming love between mama and himself but the more I listened to what he said it became clear that he only wanted something for himself. Mama didn't want this orchard. She hated the orchard and she hated the man who left it to her. But daddy wanted her to keep it. He didn't want her to keep it so she could be happy. He wanted her to keep it so he could be happy. Mama never told me about Samsara, so I don't know if what daddy said tonight is true. For all I know he was a good man and daddy manipulated mama into leaving him. It's clear now why those shadows haunted my room as a little girl. As daddy told the story tonight the shadows flew and danced through the room. Mama didn't want to live there. He took over her life. He led her to a place she hated, and she died there. Selfishness imprisoned her innocent love to want something his selfish love could not give. Innocent lovers like my mother want selfish people like my father to give love beyond their capabilities and all that happens is the trapping of an innocent lover inside a guilty lover's heart. The selfish lover cannot see past themselves. Dressing their actions in reasons caused by others is not being true to their own intentions. Our experiences, our actions made by the choices of our decisions. People say, "because of this…I did that…" How do you respond to a situation outside of your control? Father blamed everyone for his actions. He wasn't forced to go with Spike on the robbery which cost him his freedom. He wasn't forced to betray Liberty by having a relationship with mama. All those actions were by his free will, yet he assumes no responsibility. Mama made the choices, but her thoughts were manipulated by false perceptions presented by someone she trusted. If we make choices based on lies presented by someone claiming to be honest then we have been misled into making a decision. Mama loved daddy and she only went to the orchard because he promised her a happy ever after. Mama left Samsara and sold the house they lived in. She moved into a small studio apartment and went to work daydreaming with daddy about what life would be like outside of prison. He told me he dreamed with her until the dream became reality and once it became reality they didn't know how to live inside the dream. Living in a dream is not as easy as using your imagination. When you imagine a dream, you control it. When you live inside a dream the dream controls you. Mama got lost in daddy's imagination and when reality hit neither one of them were prepared to live inside it.

Mama snuck all sorts of comforts and treats to daddy. Food… clothes… a hacksaw. Daddy worked his charms, so Mama found happiness and pleasure with him. He had become her gravity. There was no line she wouldn't cross to move towards the dream of ever after with him. Sneaking a hacksaw to help a convicted killer escape conviction has to be a blinding attraction that seeks to obtain the missing pieces of self, lost to insecurity. Mama didn't get the job at the prison to break a convicted killer out. She didn't get the job at the prison to find a lover. Mama got the job at the prison because she needed money to support her new life with her husband. How does a person go so far from their original path of intentions? Love and desire. What courtroom in society would feel sorry for mama and excuse her actions in working to help a convicted killer escape from prison? Mama is looked upon as criminal for that. Pleasure and happiness lead a person from their original intentions to a place they never intended to be. The seducer decides the seductions destination. Do I believe daddy planned to lead mama down this path? It's clear from my life on that orchard that daddy's intentions were planned. My stomach turned as he drank the whisky and told the story of how he and mama got to the orchard. My repulsion for him reached a new distance between us. The flying shadows flew higher and higher towards the night sky as he spoke. The answers I'd always wanted from "did you love mama?" became clear when he mentioned the hacksaw. Still, I listened more and more to him talking about having mama break him out of prison hoping what I formulated in my thoughts about his story wasn't true. I wished Somehow the part I wanted to hear in the story would come and daddy would give the hacksaw back. His case would be overturned on appeal and he and mama would retire to the land left to her by her father. Aberration finds us so easy when we are faced with things we don't want to see. You don't disappear when I close my eyes but if I try hard enough to imagine you're gone I may be able to escape the reality that you're still there. Daddy used that hacksaw on the barriers of his confinement and one night he escaped from captivity. He said mama stashed a rope and blankets by a drop site. Daddy used the thick wool blankets to cover the barbwire on top of the prison wall he scaled with the rope. He said within 15 minutes of climbing through the window of his cell he was over the wall and outside the prison just like he and mama planned. The guards didn't notice he was gone until morning count. He'd placed pillows underneath the covers of his bed. On the top pillow, he placed a wig which matched his hair. Mama had snuck that to him too. To cover up his breakout point he put quick drying cement bonding on the portions he'd cut from the bars. He put them back into place and left with the glue still drying. The bars looked as if they'd never been touched. It would be hours before they'd knew he was gone. Mama came to pick him up from a location they'd picked twenty minutes away from the prison. Some bushes right off the main roads. He was wearing regular clothes and had shed all traces of prison. He laid down in the back seat as mama drove the few hours to their well-laid plans of the future. As he told the story I felt their excitement at coming to their new life. On that night when daddy escaped from prison, I'm sure they both felt a sense of triumph. As they headed towards their dreams of life on that land, they had no idea a nightmare was in store for them. The shadows which flowed through my room as a child didn't return to the ground from which they came tonight. The shadows flew from my room and disappeared into the night sky. How we got to the land was no longer a mystery.

Daddy told me about his misery living on the orchard alone. Mama couldn't live there for almost a year. As an escaped convict daddy's face was all over the news. He was afraid to leave the house. In his foolishness and manipulation, he'd exchanged one prison for another. My mama fell under scrutiny at the prison. Investigators knew of her close relationship with daddy. They questioned mama for hours trying to see if she knew anything that would help them locate and capture him. Mama and daddy found a new world inside the reality of their delusions. Rendezvous were too dangerous. Mama would be thrown in jail if the investigators found daddy living on the orchard. Just getting food and supplies to him was a risk in discovering their illegal activity. Mama would have supplies sent to the orchard every other month from a credit card with a fictitious name. The land was in her father's name. Their first night together, the night of the escape, Daddy said that night was the climax of their dreams. They had triumphed and reached what they believed to be destiny. Making love holding each other close and tender all through the night receiving what they'd dreamed of and then the morning came, and the dream was over. Mama departed that morning and walked into the reality of their situation. She wouldn't be coming back for at least nine months and during that nine-month separation the stresses and strains turned the orchard into a prison and their daydream into a nightmare. By the time mama made the transition to living on the farm, her and daddy were like strangers. He didn't really want to be with her. He just used mama to get out. He really only wanted Liberty. In his selfish move of manipulating my mama, he didn't see the end result until he was trapped in his own lie of wanting to live on the orchard. The next visit was different than the first. The stress of their situation had brought them down. Daddy said he asked mama if she wanted him to turn himself in. My sweet mama wouldn't let him do that. They'd come too far to turn back. At nineteen-months, the heat was dying down and it was time for mama to quit working at the prison. She'd saved up money and would live another six months away before moving to the orchard with daddy.

His selfish dream, his fake phobia. We all became prisoners because of his life on the run. He wanted to be free so bad that he didn't see the outcome of his actions. Blinded by a finish line. He didn't see the prize awaiting him. My mama loved him, and she gave her life to him when he really didn't want it. He needed to feed off her life to save his. If he could have, he would have left her, but he didn't have any place safe to go. Mama turned the orchard into a successful business which fed our family. Daddy just lived off the success. All those shadows which came out of the ground at night when I was a child represented all the questions he answered tonight. His fear of leaving the house wasn't just a phobia, it was a reality. As I drove away from that place tonight, I knew my curse had been lifted. Daddy fell asleep talking about Liberty and when he finally went quiet, I realized she was my Liberty too. That's why I came here, Rob. I want to move in with you and start our life together. I brought my dog and most of my things. He can live in the prison he created for himself. I'm done with that place.

A TALK WITH SHHH

Justus

"Squawk! Swooooos.... squawk swooos squawk!"

My heavy eyelids were hard to open. The first thing I saw through the blurry haze of sleepy vision was Shhh doing his little dance. Bobbing his head he moved side to side, lifting one foot up with one foot down. His dance of mockery.

"Shut up bird! Shut up! You're always making noises when I'm sleeping! Faith! Faith, come get this bird. Bring his night cloak. Stupid animal.... Faith!"

Shhh stopped dancing and looked at me with his left eye. His head cocked a bit to the left side as if to see me better.

"Squawk! Faiths not here...Squawk! Faiths not here swooos... Not here.... Squawk... Not here... Swoos"

He continued to dance. I rubbed my eyes to open them wider.

"What? She's what? Faith!"

I cried for help. God forbid the words from this bird's beak to be true. He tilted his head to the right. I stared into his eye and saw my reflection. My face old and worn my, youthful looks lost to the years hidden behind these walls. Robbed of my prime by my own choices. I'll be damned if I grow any older, any more bitter, allowing this bird to mock me with his staring.

"Faith! Come get this bird!"

I listened for the sounds of her footsteps in the house. Nothing. We don't live in a large home. A single story two-bedroom two bath dwelling. One kitchen, and living room, one dining room and no sounds from my daughter. I held my breath and listened for any sign of Faith. Nothing. Shhh puffed his chest and raised his head.

"Squawk! You get what you deserve. Swoos…you get what you deserve…squawk!... what you deserve. Swoos." My pill bottle hit his cage.

"Shut up your stupid bird! You don't know what I deserve. You never lived outside of a cage. How do you know what I deserve?"

"All about you. Squawk! All about you. Swoos"

I thought he looked at me through his left eye but I didn't see my reflection. So I turned around and grabbed the bottle of spirits holding his attention and guzzled the liquid until my blood boiled and I screamed.

"You don't know anything about me bird! I had a life before I got trapped here with you. I didn't want you. I didn't want any of this! I was happy with Liberty and the life we started together. You don't know. I drink because I'm in hell. From prison to here I've been in hell. Do you think I dreamed about being here? Do you think I wanted to spend the rest of my life inside a house living on an orchard? I had dreams of living life in the city and raising a family with Liberty. When I first moved here, I didn't think I'd never be able to leave. The months I spent here waiting on Hope to come join me I dreamed about being able to travel the world. Not once did I consider this as my end. So how do you know me bird?"

I reached for my bottle of whiskey. Once I got my hand on the bottle, I gripped it tight. I squeezed even harder before I tilted it to my mouth. The tasty substance cruised down my throat and soothed me; as always, it warmed my body from head to toe. The spark of life.

"Your foolish bird. You only imitate the thoughts and ideas of those around you. You don't even understand what you're saying. Like my body's reaction from too much of this liquor, you regurgitate, you vomit the accumulation of too many words listened by your ears. You don't know the pains and woes of any man. You can't even comprehend the words you speak. You only annoy and perform for those around you. "

He fluttered his wings and clamped his beak around one of the cage bars. I'd spent years in prison… years in this prison of my own making. Only to sit here yelling at a bird for an audience of conversation. My Hope is gone, and I don't know where my Faith is? How could I have expected her to stay here and live as a servant tending to my needs. This self-imposed exile was not Faith's sentence to bear.

"A pack of smokes. Squawk! A pack of smokes! Swoos"

The bird alerted me to a pack of cigarettes sitting on the nightstand. My Faith…. I grabbed the pack. To my delight a full fresh unopened box of cigarettes. A piece of folded writing paper sat underneath it. Shhh fluttered inside the cage. "Squawk…squawk!"

My heart rate increased tenfold just looking at the paper. I already knew what it said.

"Squawk!"

"Shut up bird!" He fluttered his wings.

"The truth shall set you free! Squawk! The truth shall set you free Squawk!"

I didn't want to touch it. My head throbbed. My hand trembled. The paper made a noise like flapping in the wind. Maybe my intoxication had got the better of my thinking. I could barely separate the fold.

"Squawk!"

"Shut up!"

Finally, I got it opened:

Daddy, I can't stay here any longer. After hearing what you told me tonight, I can't understand why mama stayed here so long. I don't know why she loved you beyond all measure. You only love yourself. All she received from you was selfishness. You only love yourself. You can't think past your own needs to see anyone else's. You expect me to never leave this house, and take care of you? It's not my fault you can't leave this house. It's been over 26 years and you believe you are entitled to be taken care of? While you were telling the story I wondered, were you thankful when I was born because you could raise me to take care of you? I came back tonight wanting to leave and I left here knowing I should be gone. You made this place a prison for your family. I won't stay here and finish this time with you. It's not my responsibility and I will not allow you to manipulate me like you did mama. When you are all alone, remember the woman, you watched die in front of this house. I will never forgive you for that and I will not be coming back. May God have mercy on your soul. Sincerely, Faith.

I looked up to see Shhh doing his dance. "Squawk! Just me and you! Squawk! Just me and you! Swoos…"

He was right. We were trapped here together in this prison. My Faith somewhere hating my existence while I lay here dying with Shhh. I thought after hearing the truth she would understand my illness as a condition of circumstance but all she heard was I never loved her mother. Why did it take me this long to hear it? Day after day Hope sat here with me and wasted away into nothing.

Faith heard what I couldn't. In my bitterness and self-pity, I felt my needs came before Hope's. It makes sense that this bird and I will be left here to rot and die. Faith can't see my pain. She only sees my sorrow as self-inflicted and my sweet, loving Hope as a casualty of it. Hope didn't want to be here. I wanted to live here. How is this not the life I'd always wanted when the whole time it's been my idea?"

"Squawk! What did she want? Squawk!"

Shhh danced while he spewed more words of nonsense. How do I answer his questions while keeping my sanity? He doesn't listen to my words with intentions of comprehending my answers to his questions. Why should I humor…"

"Squawk! What did she want!? Squawk! What did she?"

"Stupid animal! Quiet your noise!"

"Squawk! What did she want? Squawk! Swoos. What did she want? Squawk! She want? Swoos!"

"QUIET! In my last moments of life, why am I forced to be tortured by the sounds of your beak? No silence or peace for my life even in the last breaths of oxygen from this stale air around me. This house…this cursed land of oranges growing by the thousands. When I was a kid, oranges tasted like the sweet heaven of freedom from the city. In this house, I awake day after day looking at these trees growing around my prison. Water mixing with the soil and nutrients sucked in a concoction through roots and branches to form these orange balls of citrus year after year. My hate at the sight of this budding fruit has no bounds. My taste buds no longer crave the representation of another year in my life gone by and still this harvest comes, and I walk outside. I came here after harvest."

"Squawk! Squawk! What did she want? Squawk! What did she want!? Swoos!"

When we got here Hope told me I'd just missed seeing the trees filled with fruit. The gripping throes of disappointment met me here the first day. All those trees not bearing the fruit of my dreams. I long to see the next harvest. Our work reaped a beautiful bounty. I was so happy and then Bloom after bloom my dreams as a child became the nightmares of my adult reality. A window or open door leading outside gave vision to my reality. I'm going to die looking at my dreams live outside. What future could Hope have in a place like this? What answers can I possibly give to satisfy Faith? That's the thing, it doesn't matter now. All I can do is talk about Hope to these walls and the ears of a bird. The final breaths of my life shall be spent thinking out loud and no other person shall hear me. Have I already died? A living dead man on this orchard grave since my feet touched its grounds. All people who witnessed my life before now view me as only a memory. I told Faith the truth... tonight. How many dead men can say they were present and alert at their eulogy? Bird I'm going to do us both a favor and leave you here alone with your questions. Your words can bounce off the walls as you starve to death, smelling the stench of my body's decomposition. One thing for certain I will know right before my death, you spent your final breaths tormented by me and my final thought. *How's that for a response?* You can squawk your questions to my minds last thoughts. Before you die you'll know Hope wanted the same thing we all want. The freedom to enjoy our lives without the oppression of aching desires. Do you hear me bird? Answer me. Who lives out all their thoughts without suppression and suffering? Like Hope we want and want so many things we can't have. Even you Shhhh..."

"Squawk!"

"You sit here day after day and dance for treats and favored attention. You represent the masses of life who worship masters and lords of society who control desires with laws and advertisements as easily as I feed you treats from my hand. My Hope danced, my Faith danced, and I danced the painful movements of desires that couldn't be had. Tonight I admitted I was selfish in the actions and activities that got me to this place but who doesn't think about themselves during the contemplation of their desires? Am I to be ashamed for thinking about myself? Who am I supposed to live for if not for me? Even if I sacrifice my life for another that choice is still made by my thoughts. In choosing to live or die I am selfish in my thinking. Finding pleasure in dedication or even sacrifice we are inside our desires. Hope didn't come here by force and she didn't stay as a hostage. At any time she could have walked away or turned me in. She didn't want to be without me. I tried to push her away. We spoke countless times about letting me make the sacrifice for her to live out her years without this oppression, and time after time she told me not to do it. Should I have just walked away from this home without Hope's knowledge? Would that have made a difference? Turning myself in would've left her alone. Nobody sees that point of view. Does my daughter see her mother's choice to stay and live out her years in this house with us as a family? All my life I have been cursed with a perception at odds with everyone else's. Spike, Hope, Liberty, the jury, Faith and even you Shhh. When Hope and I fell in love I lost Liberty. My feelings have never been without remorse. I have never been free to feel without my own perspective condemning me. Loving Hope and loving Liberty at the same time, unable to choose one, I lost them both. No one sees my perspective and so it's fitting that no one will even see me when I die. No tears. No funeral of mourners crying at my passing. The only thing that will feel my departure is you, bird. You have recorded my years and for that, you are cursed to die in a cage. Even if I wanted to I couldn't stand up to let you out. In my final moments of life, I'm reduced to a crawl. Do you see my empty pill bottle on the floor? Maybe someday when we are found someone will feel sorry for us. The tragic story of a dead man and his dead bird.

"Squawk! Squawk Swoos! Never be alone. Swooos we'll never be alone. Squawk!"

"You stupid animal. How can we never be alone? Do you see anyone else here with us? Again, pointless words spill from your beak. Do you even know what never means? We live our lives as individuals. The things around us aren't who we are. Being alone is relative. Being alone in a house isn't the same as being alone in the city. Quaint surroundings make our limitations in reality unique. Maybe you're right and There is no such thing as alone, bird. The civilization of humanity exists outside that door and I refuse to step past the frame to exist with society. My footprints on earth have led me to this position, this place. My reality is here in this room with you. This place. Maybe you have some sense and I'm the one who doesn't understand. You say we'll never be alone. Together you and I we are never alone. I think I hear you, bird. The truth about being alone is in how you feel. We weather the storms of day to day activity; emotions in response to thoughts and ideas that cross our minds, the things that initiate the motions that direct our movement's. A person in a room filled with people can feel alone. A person locked in a dungeon cell can feel as if they are not alone. A state of mind holds us in the beliefs of our options. We think according to the choices we believe we have by ourselves without anyone else.

"When they find us here along with this rotten fruit they will harvest our dead corpses from this room and put us into the earth where we belong."

"Squawk! Squawk!"

"How can you dance for treats? It's the end of your life and your ignorance holds you enthralled with ritual for favor."

"Squawk! Finish your bottle... Squawk, Finish your bottle.... Swoos.... Be a good boy Justus. Be a good boy finish your bottle. Swoos... Your bottle... Squawk!"

"Quiet your noise! See, look I have already finished my bottle. You watched me when I crawled off the bed. You know where I was going and what I was going to do, bird. Believe me when I tell you Shhh, my bottle is empty and the medication is inside me already starting to do what it was made for, relieve the pain of this life. I'll take my last breaths right here on this floor. I thought I'd make it back to the bed, but my strength and my pain have reduced me to the ground. You're locked in your cage dancing for treats and telling me to finish my bottle. This whiskey has no more swallows, but cheers to you. Nighttime is over, and a new day is upon us. My last sunrise and the light still looks the same."

"Squawk! Squawk! Good morning! Squawk! Rise and shine! Squawk! Good morning!"

LOVE'S REFLECTION: WHAT IF? I WONDER...

Faith

"Rob gives me the insight to see past limitations and obstacles. We've been up all night. I feel bad for focusing on daddy's selfishness. I don't have to like what my father has done to see his side of the story. People who do things with malicious intent in their thoughts are intentionally trying to cause others harm. People who operate under the error of their ways are only at fault for being foolish. My father has made many foolish mistakes which have led him to the place he is today. He never looked farther ahead than the task at hand. Not thinking about the risk to his future lead, him to get in the car with Spike. Where would he be without that error? Does it matter? The possibilities of what if are endless. The truth of a situation is reality, the results of our choices are what we live. Hope and Justus made me. My father didn't hate my mother. She was his light in a very dark place. Two people living separate nightmares wishing together they could create a dream. We don't see the personal fantasies of the strangers we pass during our day to day activities. Who can judge the aspiring desires of a wandering soul? I condemned my father based on my own beliefs. To put my ideas against someone else's is cause for debate. We argue back and forth the notions we oppose and Then we come to resent our opponents during battle because we fought them for our love in wars. Do we have to confront ourselves to face our disagreements? Seeing my parents interact didn't feel like love. After hearing their story, I don't think they knew love. Maybe daddy thought he loved mama in the beginning, but he didn't. When he told Liberty about his prison affair with mama he was misguided by guilt. Confused by misunderstanding emotions he thought the reflection he cast on mama was love. What he failed to realize in that moment with Liberty was that he was with love. My ability to see is sometimes clouded by my notions of what I think should be. Only when I allow do my thoughts open beyond my previous perception.

We've been up all night looking for Liberty on the computer and I can't believe we found her. Amazingly she lives close by. It seems as if people are magnets in a way, drawn to each other by an unknown force. I wonder sometimes are the people in our lives by coincidence or do we coexist in a web of meaning? I have been around people who influence my choices, my courses of action and don't believe it was an accident of nature which brought these people into my life. Do I believe God controls all of us and makes us do what we are supposed to do? No. No. Watch, God doesn't dictate our movement. What fun would that be for a god? We have a higher power which created all we know, and the energy of that power is a part of us and all around us. Many of us live parallel to each other but that doesn't mean we feel the same. Our resembling does not take away our individuality. My father and Liberty have been near each other for almost twenty years without knowing it. She married a man a few years after fathers escape and then moved upstate from the city. Liberty's husband recently passed away- natural causes. How's that for irony, Watch? Two connected lives separated by pain, existing apart in a similar fashion. Liberty and her husband have a daughter together. I wonder if their daughter knows anything of father? Rob said, 'don't be surprised if you find that Liberty's daughter is just like you''. I wanted to see her face, but I couldn't find a picture of her online. I don't know how she could possibly fancy the same things as me. Yeah, like her father broke out of prison too. She just found out her father had been lying to her for 26 years too. Yeah, that's a laugh. Rob's usually right about things but about this I think he's wrong. Honestly,

I'm only doing this whole thing to prove a point. Why would Liberty want to go with me to see a man she left almost 30 years ago? The information we found on her shows she moved on with her life. He's my father and I don't want to go and see him. Rob says she won't feel the same way. I doubt it. She left him before I was born and now, I'm in the car driving to her house with you Watch, wondering what I'm going to find. Rob said, calling wouldn't be a good idea and neither would bringing daddy by. He also said, love never goes away and that love is always there, generation after generation waiting to be found by two or more. We don't control it, we don't own it. Love is there simply for all of us to enjoy. It thrives on itself generating power. The energy of love must be held reflective for its growth between people and it holds no bounds for how much it can grow. But Holding on to love by yourself is painful. Love hurts the individual who holds it alone. Daddy and mamma held love like a secret treasure chest that neither one of them could open. Did Liberty hold love all this time without a reflection of it? Rob says she did. He thinks Liberty always loved daddy and daddy's betrayal left them both holding a treasure that couldn't be spent or shared. Rob said, think about the strength it took for her to stay with him after being sentenced to life in prison. She could've been with another man and left him but she chose to stay. Only love could make that level of sacrifice. We don't pick who we find love with. We just discover it together.

What's funny about all this is I have a great sense of humor, despite growing up in a home with very little laughter. As a teenager, I can't remember too many times my parents laughed together. After being gone for a while you should walk back into your childhood home and the walls should play recollections of good times in your thoughts. It's funny I can't remember one day that we all smiled as a family enjoying time together. That used to make me so mad at Daddy, but what really made me mad was at college seeing images on television of boys and girls living in a neighborhood playing with other children. It didn't seem real to me. Neighborhoods with kids playing catch and hide and seek seemed like a fantasy. Imaginary friends and real animals like you Watch, played the part as my neighborhood when I was growing up. I had fun and didn't feel like anything was wrong, but when I got to college I found that I missed out on experiences that all my peers seem to share. Our formative years are part of our era in humanity. When my friends in college recalled old hairstyles, clothes styles and trendy sayings of their teenage experience I always felt left out. Pictures of their family reunions, weddings, graduations, and holiday celebrations made me sad because those are experiences I did not have. My friends in college had pictures which looked like the families on TV and their stories weren't made up from the fiction of their deepest desires, like mine. I used some pictures I found online and made up family history so I'd have something to say when asked. My life as a child didn't contain pictures of fun times laughing with aunts, uncles, grandparents, cousins, mom and dad. Those born into those families seemed so lucky to me. Later I found I was not alone. The more I asked about members of their families in pictures the more I discovered that no family is like TV I'm cynical now of people's lives that appear perfect. What's perfect? All the people in the world come from a mother and a father. Our worst people and our best people come from parents. You can think about the most horrible person on earth and they come from a mother, a father, grandparents, great grandparents. In some strangely complex way, we are all related. Even you have a family, Watch. All your yapping every time you hear your name. Silly dog. You probably understand love better than all us stupid people, huh boy? You stick your tongue out and wag your tail quickest I can snap my fingers. You tap right into love. When I look in your eyes, I can see it and know that when you look into mine you see it too. One thing I know for sure is love doesn't have any preferences. You can be anything and find love with something else. It doesn't discriminate. Love can form a family, but a family doesn't always form love. It's crazy how that works. Expectations are the reason I find disappointment. When you expect things to be a certain way and they're not you're let down and no one likes to be let down but still, we continue to carry expectations. I always felt my family life should be a certain way and it was only when I realized that no family is perfect that I let go of what I wanted my family to be. Letting go of how I think things should be helps me look at how things are. We fantasize about what we want and expect what we want to not be a fantasy. What we want something real. Rob says this drive will lead to the closure I need. He told me if I try to walk away from dad without looking back, I will never see myself. As much as I'd like to say this journey is about a good deed it's not. When Rob told me, I was walking away from seeing myself I felt a panic set in. My pride wouldn't let me acknowledge that in the moment he was right, but still I got up and drove to this house. All my life I'd dreamed of the day I'd be free from daddy and when I finally was I found myself no freer than when I was living in that house. Rob said I'd be better off living there versus carrying the ghosts of our home everywhere I go. Yeah, Watch, we can't hold love captive and make it what we want it to be. This woman named Liberty awaits me and somehow, she's become my salvation. Maybe her daughter will be here. I can only pray that the end of this drive will grant me the freedom I've been searching for. Well, here we are. This is the address. Maybe what Rob said will be right. Come on Watch, let's go.

LIBERTY IN THE PUZZLED WORLD
Liberty

I've looked strange place after place trying to find a mirror so I can picture the shattered pieces of myself. I tried to glue my heart back together like a puzzle using the imperfect parts that I found in the rubble of my life. Without an image to reflect on I became gripped in the frustration of why the only pieces available were a mismatched mess that only fit together by force. After years of sewing and stitching myself together I got a picture that almost looks like I used to. Mirrors are not natural. Your true vision lives in the world around you and all, I see is an endless maze of possibilities. Those choices decided my reflection. This dizzy perception. Similar to love. The peace to my puzzled world lives in the touch between a kiss. The space in-between here and there has been all I ever cared for.

We can capture love from nothing and receive love from somethings but to make it disappear takes destruction. I touch and feel with the passion of my substance and here my energy dwells seeking to be embraced and absorbed like a current.

Justus came to me in the form of flesh as a child but even before we met I felt the energy of his presence around. Living by war-torn alleys patrolled by authority I seen Justus amongst the vandals. His existence ran through the streets of my neighborhood among the rest of the children. He dreamed his life into a picture of reality against the nightmare of unending circumstances. Monsters blinded by greed and poverty. Drug-induced zombies fueled from the energy of desperation. The streets seemed to have no end twisting and turning into an empty abyss of darkness. Being in love is like holding on and letting go at the same time. Justus and I found love in the midst of a trial for our lives. The indictment against us being alive in a place where some wanted us dead. The judgment… what happens when the person you trust with your heart lies to you by breaking a promise? How do you listen when the person talking to you is a liar? Am I a fool for believing in something that might not be true? I trust. I love. I care about a person who hasn't been honest. How am I supposed to share with someone who's deceitful? Should I have excused the mistrust and listened to my heart? Listening to my mind when my heart was hurting I made a choice I didn't plan on making. For years and years, I missed the voice, the touch, and the caring of someone I never stopped loving. No matter how hard I tried, no matter how hard I wished, I couldn't stop being in a painful place with no forgiveness. My actions defined my experience and expressed my mind. I didn't choose to forgive. We attract what we find, or, is what we find attracted to us? When I left Justus, I searched to find the missing piece to my puzzle. A desperate search for something new. I went through the woes of a trial looking for jubilation as a victory. After Justus, I found Dream. Dream came when I no longer believed that a fantasy could become reality. We met under the night sky. Stars on a clear night shined upon us. The emotion of a place and time matter. I am matter. He was matter. Here's what's the matter. Looking around with nowhere to go. Dream showed me all that I had been denied by Justus. Colors seemed brighter and songs seemed wiser and over time I became the liar. Words mean nothing without actions and our desires are not blind.

Surrounded by our truths we filled our minds with beliefs. My Dream could not give me what I wanted. My heart, my indirection, my destination here years away from being back where I started. Year after year I missed knowing Justus because I matched one lie with another. I ran from love with nowhere to go. The stars in the sky shine brightly for us both in different places at the same time. How could I run in a circle and be surprised when I find myself with that which I left. My Dream did all that could be to pacify my needs, and though I meant to give my best, it wasn't enough at the end. The alarm rang and I woke up.

How do I stand before a court of my peers without tears, admitting the fears of my honest declarations that no happiness came from my dreams' recreation of Justus? Who doesn't wish, who doesn't cling to the thoughts of having simple things that comfort life? A home, a good job, vacations in different parts of the world. I didn't but some people said I had it all. What they didn't know, my Justus isn't like my Dream.

Here's the stage: We are characters brought to life through pleasure and pain. Dying twice in one life is rebirth. Old life, giving way to the new. When you see lustful eyes in the person you love, and those eyes are not for you, you may die, but you can live again when you understand that life wasn't for you. I died when the perception of my lover wanting to be with another took how to be away from me. I was smothered alive by what I believed, deceived into assuming a false identity. I died, and at birth, I cried. Born alone I lived through the hunger and thirst growing year after year as an orphan in foster care. My Dream adopted me.... and mistakes broke my ideas of perfection. Lesson after lesson my errors made my confessions. Bad days and good days filled with ideas and things I wish were a different way. So, I say as a performer in a play be serious about a life that's make-believe; own your character and at the same time be true so you can have an audience who believes the character is you. Reciting words written in the record of minds. I produced from sins the lines in the part I described. Audience of spirit excuse me. I hate to live a lie. Being reborn on stage means this life isn't about the actor it's about a great performance in the part I play. Looking at this old brand-new thing owned by life without tangibility. I ask myself how can something be lost when it's already been discovered? No matter how many times it's found this thing is more beautiful than before. A kiss, a touch, I can't believe I'm in love. Standing in its aura. Blinded by light until it's broken into colors. Deeper and deeper I go. No matter how far I reach inside I only glance back to see steps behind. It's love. Brand new wonderful love. It's a hug when I'm afraid I'll never be touched. I want to soar high and fly where love never dies. Record in the breath of life something old I keep seeing for the very first time but since I lost it, I treat it like I've never had it. I try to deny it and its ever-changing presence so easy to get confused, get bruised then sore from wrestling with something which shouldn't be ignored.

This road twists and turns with scenes of déjà vu. I've been on this street. This highway, thousands of times. Now I find it leading to answers from questions on my mind. Nothing can multiply a punishment already endured but living with actions that cannot be sure. My Dream tried to pacify my lonely sentence of life and for a long time, everything seemed to be alright. For years I satisfied myself with some else's time and in the end, I found mine disappearing. Fearing the worst, I did what I was supposed to do. Pursue the best excelling in a world of stress. Nothing less than the highest anxiety in performing for society. PTA meetings, church socials, volunteer work, always the first to raise my hand. Please understand my demand for distraction was only the symptom of a lonely life sentence. Someone has written the part and now I say the lines. The audience applauds as I do what it takes to define and represent a lie. The truth about me was not my dream. Many days I apologize for being in a place that wasn't made for me. I lived with somebody else's dream and my dream lived in someone else's place. When my Dream passed away, I stayed locked in my home. Reality was not the same with my fantasy gone. I prayed for forgiveness because not only had I lost Justus, I was in someone else's Dream. Day after day I have pleaded for redemption to find me. And today the doorbell rang. It was Faith. So now with Freedom close by my side, we go to the place where Justus resides. The power of love can forgive an error and replace a terror with happiness forever. Here driving through an orchard. No more worries. l will soon be with Justus, accompanied by the Freedom I love and this lovely Faith.

LOVE INSIDE A CAGE

Justus

"Squawk! You can have what you don't want! Squawk! Have what you don't want. Swoos! Squawk!"

Pulled from slumber, I'm still not dead. I'm still here with this stupid bird.

"How do you know bird? How the hell do you know? All you have ever wanted is snacks, water, and a place to perch."

"Squawk! How do you know? Squawk how do you know? Swoos what I want? Squawk what I want? Swoos swoos squawk!"

"What do you mean how do I know? I'm the one who feeds you and tends to your squawks and tweets. I'm the one who makes sure your cage is clean. How do I know? In that cage Without me bird, you have no life. I'm a god to you. You sing, and you dance for me. How do I know?"

"Squawk! How do you know? Squawk! How do you know? How do you know? Swoos! Swoos. Squawk."

"It doesn't matter. What could you possibly want that I don't know? You want some more food, or your cage cleaned? What! Do you want to fly out in the living room? What! Speak to me.

"Go outside! Squawk! Go outside! Swoos! Squawk!"

"We always want what we don't have, bird. Shhh. Your name is my wish. We can't have everything we desire, and we always want what we don't have. You know nothing about going outside and yet to be outside this house is your request? You stupid bird you're just as dumb as all of these silly people, wishing for things they know nothing about. I knew a guy who wished for a fancy sports car. He was a hustler in the city streets. He did what he had to for money. He had no single hustle. He went wherever the money was. I looked up to him as a role model. A man who'd been taking care of himself since he was 14 years old. He always knew the right things to say. When he was talking people wore a smile on their face. The neighborhood police didn't harass him. To me as a kid, a guy like that had everything. What could he want? A pretty girl? He had that. Nice clothes? He had that. A car? He had that, but he wanted a better one. He hustled hard to get a new car. He'd say, "almost there" when I walked past him getting his hustle on. Then one day he got the car. It was a shiny red 2 door sports convertible. It was the nicest in the neighborhood. Unlike all of them who wished for things without working, he wished for something and worked until he got it. A brand-new car. The cops didn't like it and stopped smiling like he had spat in their faces. Here was a hustler they'd let get something better than they could afford. People who used to smile because they were happy to see him now only smiled because of what they could get from him. He and his girlfriend broke up because he cheated on her. The guy who used to make all the people smile was now the guy who made a lot of people frown. Two months after he bought his brand-new car, late at night he was at a gas station when some stick-up kids from another neighborhood tried to rob him. He never gave me the details of what happened. He just said it was all so fast. One minute he was whistling, walking out of the store and the next he was laying on the ground paralyzed from the waist down. Even though he can't drive his car anymore he probably still has it. When I left the neighborhood, he would wash it and wax it like he was going somewhere but all he'd do is look at it. He finally got what he wanted. His brand-new shiny sports car. I always wondered what made him want it. He gave up everything for a dream created by someone else. He wasn't born wanting it. He didn't design it. Someone else made his fantasy from start to finish. He got the car he wanted, and he never drove another car again.

Why aren't we satisfied with the things we have, bird? Look at you. You want to go outside your cage and outside this house into the wind in any direction you choose for as far as you can fly but you don't know what's really out there. You only dream in your foolish ignorance about what lays outside that door. A cat may be waiting by the trees when you least expect it. Maybe an alligator is where you go to get a drink of water. How about a snake? You'll land right next to him thinking the branch is safe and then smack! You only conjure happy thoughts of life outside your prison cage. You want to sing with birds who might wish you harm because of fantasies created in your imagination. The things outside your body are not yours. All you have is with you. Who you are is what you are at any time day or night. I should let you have your past the front door. A 26-year-old bird that has never been outside killed his first day in the real world. – News at 11. Now. That's funny.

"Squawk! Squawk! Swoos."

"It's cold in here huh?"

"Squawk! Cold. Squawk! Cold. Swoos."

I agree with you there, bird. This house is always cold. Always. Always! Always cold and miserable. You're lucky you have never known love, bird. You don't know what it's like to hold something you want to express and not be able to share it. Even expressing love to a person who doesn't love you is better than being in love with someone you can't even talk to. At least there's a chance for courtship when you profess your undying devotion day after day. After finding love with someone and sharing it with them nothing else can compare. This house is the perfect metaphor for what that leaves behind. A cold hollow place where even with people feels empty. Being left alone with love you die and still breathe, walking the earth like a zombie searching the world for anything that can sustain the rotting corpse of your life with more than wishes and regrets. This home could be 100 degrees and still feel cold. The chill tickles your bones and never touches the skin. The goosebumps I used to feel when she was near have hardened all sense of touch now that she has gone. I am tired of avoiding the truth. Some would say this was better than prison and it was. I should have appreciated it more. Living on an orchard with a pretty woman and beautiful child is a fantasy most men never get to experience and yet every day I lived here in misery. Only a fool like me would realize this when it's too late. I can feel the pills working again Shhh. It's almost over. I should have done this long ago and freed this house from my curse of the cold.

"Squawk! Faith? Squawk! Faith? Swoos Squawk!"

…She's gone. Faith's gone. Hold onto something tight and if it breathes you will constrict its energy for life. After the fall Faith just never came back to me. She never understood how I could stand there and watch her suffer because of my fears. Faith has the belief that love goes beyond the fears that hold us back. Stories of mothers finding the strength to lift cars off their children are examples that validate her beliefs about my love. I have wanted Faith to understand that I didn't abandon Hope outside. There were just people around Hope and I couldn't get past my fears of them and what they'd think to be with her. I lost Hope and once that happened losing my Faith was the only fear I had left. Nothing else mattered to me but Faith and she hated me without understanding who I am. I figured if I could endure through the punishing persecution every day, someday Faith would see my devotion and reward me for how I suffered with open arms and no question. Hope knew what I wanted, and she'd always say…

"Squawk! Around someday. Squawk. Someday. Swoos."

"Yeah, I know you've heard Hope say that countless times over the years. When Faith would rebel and reject me Hope would say how far is someday away from today? I thought Faith would come back once I made my confession, but it was the opposite effect. My confession absolved her of administering the daily persecution of my punishment. I never thought I'd miss the malediction of my Faith. My revelation only vandalized her image of me. Faith promised Hope she'd never leave, and I thought that was good enough for her to always stay here with me. I always hung on to the belief that once I told Faith the truth about me that she would understand and forgive. It's stupid to assume. I learned not to assume as a kid because nothing is promised, and everything is always subject to change. Still, foolishly I believed Faith would hear me and stay by my side. I can't see how such a thing could have held me for so long. Now I have nothing left in here. All I have is outside.

"Squawk! The last time you said I love you? Squawk! The last time Squawk! I love you Swoos! I love you. Swoos"

"…I love you too, bird. We've had some good times here. Me training you to understand me. You're my only friend and you know I'd never leave you to die in that cage. Faiths gonna be coming by to pick up the rest of her things. I don't know when, but she'll be here within a few days. She's not coming here to stay. I knew this day was coming and I knew my Faith. She won't leave without saying I love you. A long time ago I told Hope she should've left me to rot and die in prison. She told me that would've been a waste of a life because we wouldn't have Faith. Since that conversation, I've counted Faith as my only blessing and for years I have been foolish. Instead of being happy with my riches I lived pushing them away. After Faiths fall, she saw me for what I really was; a bitter man who repelled the love around him and refused to do anything to make this house a home. I rarely ever told Hope I loved her and the sound of those words from her always made me uneasy. She must have seen my body tense up at least once or twice."

"Squawk! You don't have to say it back. Squawk! Say it back. Swoos! I know you love me. Swoos. I know Squawk!"

"I do. All I could ever say is I do. I can still feel her lips kiss me when those two words left my mouth. The kisses of Hope are no longer for me to have. Here lies a man who didn't understand how to live until it was time for him to die. It's time for me to rest my eyes bird. This medication is finally working. I do Hope. I do."

THE FINAL JUDGEMENT
Faith

"Dad... Dad, are you awake? I'm coming into the room. I've got a surprise for you."

"Squawk! I love you Faith, squawk! I love you swoos."

"Daddy! How did you get on the floor?"

"Squawk! Love you, Faith. Squawk... love you."

"Shut up! Stupid bird shut up! Daddy Oh my god? Did you take all these pills? Daddy wake up!"

"Faith I'm so glad you made it. I love you and I have always loved you. I've been.... I've... I..."

"Daddy save your strength."

"I've been such a fool...All these years. Faith. I had it all. Everything a person really needs was here with us. Look over there I carved that... for you. It's what I want the world to know about Us...and what we learned here."

"That's a headstone for a grave...Daddy why?"

"You'll be able to live now Faith. Read it...Read..."

"Squawk! Read what it says! Squawk! Read what it says Swoos. I love you Faith Squawk! I love you, swoos."

"Daddy why would you do this?

"Read it Faith…please."

"The essence of life is misunderstood by those who don't understand love" …Daddy Please tell me why. Please. Everything was just starting to make sense."

"Honey…I can't hold you hostage any more. My life is only making yours worse."

"Daddy… This was supposed to be a joyous day. Why is this happening? You are supposed to be smiling right now. You have another daughter."

"What? I don't understand Faith… where did that come from?"

"Liberty. Liberty is here to see you.

"What? Liberty?"

"Yes, Justus. me."

"My God! Liberty…I never meant to hurt you."

"I know Justus. I know. Faith let me sit here with your father alone. Please. I'll call you and Free back in a few minutes."

"Okay, I've got to call Dr Keeler. Here, lift Daddy's head off the floor. Daddy. I love you."

"I love you too Faith. Everything's going to be ok."

"I know daddy. I know. I'm going to call the doctor. I'll be right outside the room."

"She's a good daughter Justus. You did a good job raising her. She loves you a lot."

"I… I messed up bad Liberty."

"No… No, you didn't Justus. You had a family and lived a good life many wish they could have experienced."

"Liberty… I made this house miserable. Every day I did all I could to demonstrate how much I hate this house. I wasn't a good father to Faith and I wasn't a good husband to Hope. I was just here wishing I wasn't."

"Oh, Justus you've always been unable to see the real effect you have on people. You think our feelings are based on the feelings from your own perceptions. Your daughter has grown up knowing you love her. There is no way she hasn't known you love her and even in all of the actions of rebellion towards you, you've always known deep down that she loves you too."

"Liberty I have not been a good father. She'd have been better off without me."

"You still can't see what's right in front of your eyes. Your daughters love for you brought me here. I'm sitting in front of the father of my child because of the love Faith has for you Justus. You are a very lucky man. Think of all the people you left behind serving life in prison. You have to see it wasn't all a waste. Your life meant something, Justus. Freedom! Freedom! Come in here."

"Freedom, who is Freedom?"

"Squawk! Freedom! Squawk! Freedom! Swoos. your daughter! Squawk!"

"You have a very smart bird. That's amazing. If I didn't know better, I'd ask him how he knows to say that!"

"I don't know how he knows but he does seem to have some sort of sense about what's going on here. He's a really good friend."

"That is so funny Justus. Your bird loves you too. Do you see that?"

"Squawk! Squawk! Swoos!"

"Huh! Uh… um…. yeah… that old bird does love me. "

"Yeah, he does. We all love you, Justus. "

"Mom, you called me?"

"Yes, Free. I want you to meet someone very special. This is your father."

"This is her?"

"Yes. Justus…. this is our daughter."

"Oh my god. What have I missed in this life? I missed your life from birth. I have missed your growth."

"Father, my love for you has always been and even as I sit before you now I don't feel you as a stranger. I have always felt you as a part of me and Mother has told me all about you."

"And did she tell you how stupid I am?"

"No…. not at first. As I grew older, she told me bits and pieces about you two growing up."

"Were you disappointed about me being your father? I always wanted you to exist."

"Dad, mom told me how important it was for you two to bring me into this world. I have never thought for one second, you'd be away from me if you knew I existed. I have always known you'd love me. Maybe that's what happened here. "

"What do you mean?"

"Oh daddy, I'm surprised you can't see what happened here. We have experienced the definition of love."

"Squawk! Squawk! Swoos."

"In two places at one time, apart from each other's worlds dad. Love is a magnet that will somehow, some way bring individuals together."

"Squawk!"

"This moment I have wished for all my life and I'm so glad that you finally get to hear me say I love you, daddy. I love you so very much."

"Liberty… We made a child."

"Yes, Justus. We have a beautiful daughter. We were always meant to be in one spirit. Look at her."

"She's beautiful. I always wondered what Freedom looked like and now I know. I see my Freedom. Faith! Where's my Faith?"

"I'm right here daddy. Doctor Keeler is on his way.'

"Oh, sweetheart. He's not going to be in time."

"Please don't talk like that. You have a lot of life left."

"No Faith don't cry. it is my time to move on."

"Daddy you don't understand. You have to see your grandchild be born."

"Oh, Faith. You will make sure my grandchildren know about me through your stories and life lessons about growing up here on this farm."

"Dad, I'm pregnant."

"What?"

"Squawk! Swoos. Swoos."

"Rob and I… we are going to get married. We found out yesterday. I'm over two months pregnant."

"I'm happy for … you and Rob… sweetheart…. ugh…. ugh…. um… Rob is a very lucky man. That is wonderful news Faith. I'm so sorry honey…. Even my last action punishes you. umm…"

"Daddy you will be here. You and your journey are not over. Dr. Keeler will be here soon."

"What… um…. what…what do you want for your child Faith?"

"Squawk! What do you want? Swoos… What do you want? Squawk!"

"Dad that bird is silly. All I want for my children is for them to see this world with love and make it better than it was before. I want to create good people."

"Faith"

"Yes, Daddy?"

"Make sure your children know, make sure they know how much you love them."

"I will daddy I promise."

"I need one more thing, Faith..."

"Yes, Daddy?" "I …I …. I …. I want you to…."

"Daddy?"

"Let Shhh fly outside. Let him out of the cage... ugh... Let him out of this house."

"Daddy! Daddy! Don't close your eyes!"

"I love you all very much. Hope I can see you now…"

"Daddy! Daddy!"

"Oh, Faith sweetheart. Let him rest. Let him rest."

"Liberty, why?"

"Close your eyes and let us pray. You two girls bow your heads in silence. He deserves peace. It's all he ever wanted."

OUTSIDE THE HOUSE

Faith

"Free, When I was a child, I wished daddy was dead. What small child hasn't had an angry thought about an authority figure? Silly Selfish wishes from a child who knows not the ways of the world. At the time, I had no idea what it would mean for my father to be dead. I just wanted to lash out with the worst thoughts imaginable. Daddy and I didn't get along very well. I'd fallen off my bike when I was a little girl and he just stood yards away and watched while I cried. It really hurt. You can still see the scars? I had stitches right here on my forehead. He'd promised me before that day that he'd always protect me. Then when I needed him, he stood there and watched me hurt and didn't move an inch to help. He broke a promise to a little girl who idolized him, and my child eyes could see nothing more in him from then on other than a liar. I didn't believe in him anymore after that and I wished he'd go away. Year after year we just grew farther apart. Now my wish has come true and he's gone. And I really wish he was still here. He didn't even find out that for the last ten years he's been a free man. I still can't believe that his old friend spike went to jail for another murder and confessed to the one daddy was convicted of. I wished that somehow, he could have seen all the people that came to his funeral today. Growing up I never saw him with any friends, so it was a shock to see so many people. His old neighborhood really loved him. It's nice Your mom was in contact with so many of them still. Our father Justus. How could I have ever wanted Justus to die? He taught us all that when we don't understand love, we misunderstand life. We can practice science and religion but only love can truly give us the experience of being. No word definitions can give us that. Daddy said that we feel life through love and no words can truly express the feeling of life or the feeling of love. I'm glad he finally felt the love of life and that we were there to feel it with him. There are things I wish I hadn't said. Sometimes I would say things to him and regret the words as they came out of my mouth. Words have a powerful effect on our lives. We can say a few words and change everything around us. The power of words has ignited countless wars, fights, and ended relations between people who once stood side by side. I'd be upset with him after our encounters and then I couldn't even remember what had set me off. It seems like sometimes I would be mad at him for no particular reason at all. I'd just carry frustration everywhere I went. Being cautious about life has never been my strong point and so I'm struggling with reckless actions that have caused regret and turned my frustration into shame.

What if all our thoughts could be read by those around us? Reading minds would have some pluses. Think of all the things you could avoid. Some stranger having thoughts of harming you could be foreseen and avoided. What could be bad about being able to stay away from danger? Well, how about seeing thoughts that will never be expressed or acted upon. You know what I mean? The things which make us cringe at the thought of them becoming real. Like wishing father was dead.

Still, it doesn't take a mind reader to know when someone you love doesn't care anymore.

It's like calling out for loves embrace to surround your heart with warmth but you only receive loves fingertips slipping away as your voice is drowned out by the object of your affection. Your love is unable to see you, unable to hear you. The audience of pain applauds for those who are invisible to the person they care for most. When we spend so much time doing what makes us feel good, satisfying our cravings, we miss the point of life and selfishly make love alone. Love must be reflective. What we know now is nothing compared to our future experiences. Our future experiences touch us and mold our beliefs. If we stay locked in a house like daddy, then we miss the experiences which live right outside our front doors. We are Social beings with a popular culture shared through customs and traditions. We thrive in the world around us making an identity based on our experiences. Being trapped in a prison is not an easy way to understand love. Under those conditions, most people seldom feel, or even come to fully understand, life/love personal definition. A person who holds love captive limits its amount of nourishing food called reflection. A love in a prison or a cage grows under the same hardship as a flower growing through a crack in the concrete of a busy walkway. The footsteps carelessly stomping around its delicate nature day and night. The flower holds on for dear life as it tries to reach for a star. Quiet Watch. He always gets excited when he hears things mama used to say. We sure did draw a lot of attention going to a funeral with a barking dog. I don't leave Watch alone. We are all that's left. …well …there is that bird. I can honestly say I'm going to miss having him in the house but we both have our freedom now. No pun intended sis, your name is really cool. Freedom. When I found out that you were my sister I realized how selfish and spoiled I must look. I got to spend time with him, but I didn't get to know him. I can recall experiences and reflect on the times we shared. When you told our father you knew you'd meet him someday, my heart sank into my stomach. I'd spent so much time rejecting a man who loved me. What a foolish thing to do. We just left him in the cemetery and I cringe at the thought, how could I have wanted daddy to die? When stress and regret keep you from sleep life seems to be suspended in animation. It took a night standing still with my thoughts to see how I mistook dreams for nightmares. Making wishes from hate can't be a dream. Evil lives outside love. A person who believes love lives in actions of destruction doesn't know loves embrace. Making things better is love and in love we can live in a place where lying awake all night only happens when we can't wait to see tomorrow. Like a wedding or a birthday…. Celebrations of life should feel like love. I have what I used to wish for and now I feel guilty for my thoughts. Evil in thought or evil in physical action?

All I learned in college and I just now understand the answer to that question. I wrote a paper on the topic in my ethics class. My paper was an argumentative essay. I wrote on both sides of the topic with a pro-opinion position for each side. My conclusion had to find a middle ground for the two opinions to agree. My conclusion to the question… is evil in thought or evil in our physical actions, went something like this:

"Our ideas, no, no, our thoughts have a place in our actions. We do things because of the choices we make. When I grab an ice cream it is because I decided to move and grab it. Are all physical actions based on our choices? Of course not. Involuntary physical movements happen all the time, but I rule out involuntary movements because they have no place in either of these opinions. How can we label involuntary physical actions from a person as that person's purposeful evil? When we make the choice to do something that choice is made from a thought in our minds.

I didn't wish daddy good will and good fortune and so my actions weren't moved towards his goodwill or good fortune. I didn't raise fists to him and beat him towards death every day but I might as well have because in my mind that's how I felt, and my actions reflected such. Every response or action I gave was based on my thoughts of hate and so even when I made dinner or spoke there was no love because of how I felt. He probably wished I would do something to finally get all my anger out instead of enduring day after day. The paper got an A+ on the subject of evil in thought or in action and just now I understand what my conclusion means. I was lucky to say goodbye to dad and let him know I love him. Think of what a person you love must feel when they die without knowing your love. I almost had to live the rest of my life regretting not telling daddy that I still loved him. We all have to meet death. Every person we see will have a day to die and that means all the people we love will someday be gone. My father lived for over twenty years knowing his daughter hated him and wished he'd go away… he killed himself to grant me that wish. I didn't have to say I want you to be no more for him to understand the thoughts in my mind. He could see in my actions towards him how I felt. Sometimes it's just a matter of being aware of someone because they feel our feelings. You don't have to look hard at a bird in a cage to know the bird doesn't want to be there. We just get used to it and ignore the fact for our own needs. I called him selfish and the whole time the selfish one was me. In a hundred years new people will be born and live on this land…well… if people are still here in this part of the world. New stories of life will be born and old stories will have been told. All my problems at home with dad will have been swept as a grain into the sands of time. Sometimes I'd argue with him, yelling and screaming at the top of my lungs and I would think how did we go from silence to yelling? To this day I can't remember how a lot of those fights started but I can remember how a lot of them ended. There were good times though. He loved to go out on his annual walk through the orchard in the moonlight. And he loved to tell stories about the city. Liberty has so many tales about daddy. He couldn't tell me the truth about his past life in the city, so when I was little, he'd tell me bedtime stories that were really about himself, and where he came from. I'm glad you and Liberty decided to stay and help with the orchard. She told me dad used to dream of living in a place like this. If only by chance or circumstance was I able to bring all of us together for his last breath I am thankful. Time with loved ones is precious… we should never waste it.

Well, here we are. Home sweet home. Oh wow, yeah, I see him too. He looks so happy up there. I thought once he got outside that cage and the house he'd fly far, far away but all he did was perch in that peach tree. He loves those peach pits. Look he's dancing. All those years he looked at that tree from his cage and now he's there. He made it. Hey Shhh! Hey Shhh! Silly bird, come down from there and get back inside."

"Squawk! Squawk! I love you, Faith. Squawk. I love you. Swooos, love you."

"Dad knew that bird was looking at that tree all of these years and he knew that bird would stay there once outside, echoing the words he trained him to say. Thank you, daddy. We are here now, and your heart is outside the cage."

"Squawk! I love you, Faith! Squawk! I love you. Swoos…"

"I love you too, Dad."

EPILOGUE

You have just read my allegory of personal involvement with Hope, Faith, and Justice. I have found that Liberty in Justice allows Hope for the future. When Justice finds Hope's sanctuary (in prison) Liberty is lost with the conception of Freedom. The escape of Justice comes with Hope, but only Faith can deliver Liberty and Freedom. When Hope dies, Justice and Faith struggle to coexist in the same place. Faith and Justice don't believe in the same things. Faith, Rob's everything, leaves Justice to be with her love and following Rob's advice brings them all Liberty and Freedom. Silence is the sound of one's own insecurities and throughout the allegory, I wrote Shhhh to reflect that.

Thank you for taking the time to experience this book. As with all my books, I write for readers to connect and grow in ways that make our world better. Remember Hope, Faith, Justice, Liberty, and Freedom when faced with the recollections found in silence. Shhh....

-Tshombe

Other works by Tshombe include:
The Fantasy of Love: The Broken Mirror
The Professor
Sarah's Diary

Follow Tshombe on Instagram at @professorsworld
to connect with the author, receive insights into his works, and
opportunities to be the first to read his newest releases for free.

www.ingramcontent.com/pod-product-compliance
Lightning Source LLC
Chambersburg PA
CBHW050801250626
47155CB00005B/2169